THE AMERICAN WIFE

Elaine Ford

THE AMERICAN WIFE

THE UNIVERSITY OF MICHIGAN PRESS

Ann Arbor

2010   2009   2008   2007   4   3   2

A CIP catalog record for this book is available from the British Library.

Library of Congress Cataloging-in-Publication Data

Ford, Elaine.
    The American wife / Elaine Ford.
        p.   cm. — (Michigan literary fiction awards)
        ISBN-13: 978-0-472-11620-1 (cloth : alk. paper)
        ISBN-10: 0-472-11620-7 (cloth : alk. paper)
        I. Title.

    PS3556.O697A44   2007
    813'.54—dc22   2007019156

ACKNOWLEDGEMENTS

The following stories in this collection originally appeared, in somewhat different form, in these publications:

"The Garage Artist." *The Boston Globe Magazine.* March 17, 1985.

"Changeling." *The Colorado Review.* Special Issue: "Going Places." Summer, 2002. Vol. XXII, No. 2.

"Dyslexia." *The Boston Globe Magazine.* April 10, 1983.

"The Cocoanut Grove." *Stand Magazine.* Summer, 1998.

"Rita Lafferty's Lucky Summer." PEN Syndicated Fiction Project. *Arizona Republic, Newsday, Miami Herald.* Summer, 1983. Reprinted in *The Available Press/PEN Short Story Collection,* 1985.

"Cousins." *Natural Bridge.* No. 5. Spring, 2001.

"The Scow." *The MacGuffin.* Special Issue: "Looking Forward . . . Looking Backward." Vol. 17, No. 2. Summer, 2000.

"The American Wife." *The Boston Globe Magazine.* November 3, 1985.

"A Sense of Morality." *Seattle Review.* Spring, 1985, Vol. VIII, No. 1.

"Red Woman, Black Woman." *Hanging Loose* 70. Spring, 1997.

"Hide and Seek." *Red Rock Review.* Spring, 1997.

"Reaping Tares." *The Nebraska Review.* Winter, 2000. Vol. 28, No. 1.

"Since You've Been Gone." *Confrontation.* Spring/Summer, 2001. No. 74/75.

For Arthur Boatin
Without whose loving help this book
would not have been possible

And for
Marian Allen, Cindy Eves-Thomas,
Naomi Jacobs, Deborah Levine

CONTENTS

THE GARAGE ARTIST

People in our village called him the garage artist because he actually lived in one, with a leaky wood stove that barely took the chill off, and in the midst of a variety of useless objects that had either been abandoned there or abandoned somewhere else and rescued by him. Not rescued for any artistic purpose, though. He was not a found-object sculptor; he did not construct collages or paint hard-edged realistic studies of rusted car mufflers, say, or three-legged kitchen chairs.

What he painted were snowscapes: precisely rendered though somewhat abstract scenes done in oils on pieces of wood that were no more than eighteen inches square. He painted snowscapes whether there was snow on the ground or it was the middle of summer. He applied the paint with thin blades set in handles. The colors he used were mostly whites and grays and ice blues, with dark vertical lines for trees. Once, though, I was startled by a small flash of crimson near the center of a picture. The carcass of an animal half-eaten by some predator? Or perhaps only a wool cap snagged from a child's head by a branch and lost. I'd learned better than to ask. The meaning was in the picture; you were supposed to figure it out for yourself.

I was ten the summer he moved into Mrs. Gapp's garage. It had once been a barn and was on the edge of her property, which made it closer to our house than to hers, with a wide grassy lane in between. Mrs. Gapp told my mother he had earned a Bronze Star in the Battle of the Bulge, and she considered it her patriotic duty to rent to him. He might be a little odd, she said, but that was only the deafness in the bad ear, the one next to which the shell had exploded. Swell patriotism, I thought to myself, taking money from a hero to let him live in a garage. But Old Hairy-Mole, as my sister Margaret called her, needed the money; apart from what her son sent, her only income came from the brown eggs she sold. Anyway, the soldier seemed happy enough.

I used to watch him walk along the lane, heading toward the village; an hour or so later he'd pass by again, carrying his groceries in a greenish knapsack. If he happened to notice me sitting on the glider on our porch, he would lift his arm in a solemn, though unmilitary, salute. I liked it that he didn't smile; I felt that this man took my existence more seriously than adults usually did.

At the end of the summer my mother and Margaret canned tomatoes. They spent two whole days plunging tomatoes into boiling water and skinning them and packing them into quart jars which they processed in the dented old sterilizer. When the jars were cool, my mother said to me, "You might as well take a couple to the soldier in the garage. Mind your manners and come straight home without dawdling."

That was the day I found out what the soldier was doing in Mrs. Gapp's garage. His brown hair, grown somewhat shaggy by then, had paint in it, and I saw a half-finished picture on his easel. He wiped his bony hands with a rag and set the two jars on a wooden counter he'd rigged up. While he was thanking me I let my glance slide along the counter. He had one saucepan, one skillet, and a mug. There was an oval enamel dishpan, chipped on its rim, but no faucet.

"Where do you get your water?" I asked.

"I pump it out of the ground." His voice was pitched low and there were spaces or pauses between each word.

"I never saw a water pump around here."

"You have to know where to look," he said gravely.

"Is that what you cook on?" I was talking about a little one-ring Coleman stove.

"That's right."

"Can you make a whole meal on it?"

He sat on a canvas cot and lit a cigarette. The cot had crisscrossed wooden legs. "Mostly I just eat eggs."

"That's not very healthy," I said, forgetting to mind my manners.

He cleared his throat. "Now I have tomatoes to eat, too."

"Well, I have to go now."

"Come again," he said.

Of course, I did. I would take him part of a cake we'd had for supper the night before, or a bunch of dried wildflowers in a scrubbed-out peanut butter jar. Sometimes I dropped in just to watch him paint. He asked me to call him by his name, Daniel. He told me, eventually, about growing up in Nanticoke, Maryland, where he used to fish for crabs. That's the thing he missed most living up north, he said: eating softshell crabs. He'd had a springer spaniel named Alice whose favorite food was salami. Once he won second prize in a spelling bee in front of the whole school. The word he missed was *hullabaloo*. He'd put four *l*'s in it. "That's one word I can sure spell now," he said. "Can't say I find a lot of use for it, though." He didn't smile, but I could tell when he was joking.

The one time I asked him about the war, hoping I'd hear what they gave him the Bronze Star for, he only said, "I didn't care much for killing." So I knew better than to ask again, just as I didn't ask about his paintings. I never found out why he painted snowscapes, when he came from a place where snow rarely stuck if it fell at all.

My sister Margaret wanted to know about the garage. What it was like inside, with the soldier living there.

"Oh, it's all old junk," I said. "Not even good enough junk for the scrap drive."

Margaret concentrated on winding a hank of her red hair around a metal curler. She was sixteen and vain about her hair. "Why doesn't he haul it over to the dump behind the hen houses?" she asked.

"He likes it. He brings back other stuff he finds, too."

"What kind of stuff?"

"Busted typewriters." I shrugged. "Old roller skates."

"What in the world for?"

"Don't ask me."

Actually, I had the idea that people's rejects were the same as stray cats to him; he couldn't bear to see them left out in the rain. Margaret would hoot if I said that, though.

"What are his pictures like?" Margaret asked when she was on the sixth curler.

"Not much in them. Just snow."

I didn't want Margaret to be interested in Daniel; he was *my* friend. But she went right ahead and fell in love with him. Looking back on it now, I suppose it was inevitable. For one thing, there was nobody else. It seemed we were all women up on our hill. Mrs. Gapp had been a widow for twenty years and her only son was married and gone; Mrs. Wallace's husband was away in Japan in the Occupation; Molly Spears had never married. There was no man in our house, either; my father had died of lung inflammation in 1939, when I was still practically an infant.

But I don't mean to give the impression that Margaret would have fallen in love with just anybody, merely for the sake of falling in love. She was hard on people, especially the boys in the village, and she could be a cruel mimic. My mother once observed that the sweetness went out of Margaret when Dad died. The only creatures Margaret gave any sign of caring about were Dad's pet pigeons. She would spend hour after hour in the backyard by their coop, which Dad had made out of used doors and other odd scraps. She warmed and tamed them in her hands. By then, of course, they weren't the same pigeons as Dad's, but their descendants. "She loves those birds better than she loves you or me or anybody," my mother said.

Until she discovered the garage artist. Oh, it was a long time before Margaret revealed in any way how she felt. But one night at supper Mother remarked that the soldier appeared to be in dire need of clothes for cold weather. She was, she said, going to sort through the boxes of Dad's clothes in the attic to see if there were any coats or jackets the moths had left in one piece.

"They wouldn't fit," Margaret said, looking down at a slice of fried eggplant on her plate. "They'd be way too big."

"Certainly they'd fit. You probably remember your father as a big man because you were such a little squirt yourself, but he wasn't at all. He was stringy and bony, exactly the same as that soldier." Mother added with a rueful laugh that seemed to have some scorn in it too, "A stiff wind would blow both of them away."

Margaret got up from the table suddenly, leaving most of her supper uneaten. I thought she was upset that Mother would think about giving away Dad's clothes. Now I realize she must have been embarrassed—stunned, even—to hear Mother discussing the body of the man Margaret loved, as matter-of-factly as a boiling fowl or a breast of veal.

Soon after that Margaret began to refer to him as Daniel. She spoke his name with such uncharacteristic care and respect that I knew she must love him. She began to go the garage nearly every day on the pretext of coaxing her pigeons down from the ridgepole, where they liked to roost, and she'd find some excuse to go inside. While she hovered about Daniel's easel, inarticulate with longing, he would just paint patiently on; he was, I now think, paying far more attention to something going on in his own head than to Margaret or me.

Last fall, while visiting my daughter in Boston, quite by accident I came upon an exhibition of Daniel's paintings. As an adjunct to a retrospective of a famous twentieth-century realist, the Museum of Fine Arts had mounted a small show of the work of this eccentrically single-minded artist. Odd, I thought, because Daniel was no realist, even though his paintings recognizably depict snow, and skeletal trees, and shadows, and once in a while something that might be a wool cap. I wanted to grab the lapels of the curator who assembled Daniel's show. "Look here," I would have said, if I'd had the nerve, "Daniel painted those pictures in Mrs. Gapp's garage under an electric light bulb. He never so much as glanced at real snow, not in a professional way. These pictures are about something else. No, I don't *know* what. You're the expert. You tell me."

The winter Margaret fell in love she was impossible to live with. She grew tenser and tauter by the day, more ill-tempered with me, more sarcastic about everything in the world that did not have to do with Daniel. Passion did not improve her looks. Her red hair sprang out of control; her skim-milky skin blotched alternately with embarrassment and distress. After a while my mother decided that Margaret's irritability was the result of a vitamin D deficiency and made her take a daily dose of cod liver oil, with a peppermint for the sake of her digestion. Month after month Margaret walked around reeking of mint and fish, entirely uncured of what ailed her.

After the garden had been harvested, and the maple leaves raked and burned, Margaret noticed that some of the pigeons were off their feed. One by one they sickened. Aimlessly they hopped around in the backyard, sad and dull-eyed. In November Margaret took the bus to Closter, carrying one of the stricken birds in a grocery carton. The vet diagnosed ornithosis. The whole flock would have to be destroyed, he told Margaret, before they infected all the domestic poultry for miles around, not to mention any people who might come in contact with them. But no callous official was going to slaughter Margaret's birds, on that she was adamant. Reluctantly the vet agreed not to notify the Board of Health if she'd promise to take care of the matter herself. "Cross my heart, hope to die," she said.

In the mood she was in Margaret might well have kept silent in spite of her promise, hoping her pigeons would recover of their own accord, letting Mrs. Gapp's chickens and her family and the neighbors take their unwitting chances. But she couldn't do that to Daniel. The person she loved most, perhaps solely, was put at risk by her own beloved birds. It must have been terrible for her.

When Margaret broke the news to us, my mother's first thought was: "How ever are we going to murder seventeen pigeons? Rat poison?" she mused, whanging at a cabbage with a butcher knife to hack it up for coleslaw. "Could we talk them into eating it?"

I looked at the knife. "We could chop their heads off," I suggested.

Margaret went out to the garage.

There had been no snow yet, but the day was bitterly cold. When Daniel and Margaret came walking back together across the lane the sun was just setting, a smear of red behind our hill. Daniel carried the metal pail he used for transferring water from the pump to the garage; I could tell from the way he walked that the pail was full.

I pulled on my coat and went out the back way. When I got to the coop, Margaret was crouched down with her head inside the hinged door, counting the pigeons. She emerged, and Daniel asked in his soft voice, "All present and accounted for?"

She nodded. Her hair was wild and her face blanched, except for the bright tip of her nose.

"You go on back to the house, then," he said to her.

She stared at him. "They're my birds," she said.

"Do as I say, Margaret."

She gave him the most furious look I'd ever seen on anyone's face. Then she turned, and we could hear her shoes crunching away across the frozen grass.

After a pause I asked, "Do I have to go, too?"

"No, you'd better stay and help."

I squeezed into the coop. It was dark in there and the ammonia smell from the droppings nearly made me faint. One by one I grabbed the sick pigeons and handed them out to him. When none were left I backed out. By the pail I saw a neat pile of wet iridescent bodies, their heads at one end of the pile and their curled pink toes at the other.

Daniel dumped the water out into the grass and heaped the pigeons into the pail, quite gently, considering they weren't feeling anything. Then we went to the place behind the hen houses and blackberry brambles where Mrs. Gapp deposited her trash, and we buried the little corpses in the cold cindery soil.

So far as I know, Margaret never went to visit Daniel in the garage again. In the spring she graduated from high school and found a job in an insurance office in Closter. The following summer she married her first husband, whom she'd met on a blind date. Daniel lived in the garage seven or eight more years, painting more snowscapes and collecting more junk, until Mrs. Gapp died and the people her son sold the property to had the garage torn down and the lot subdivided. By then I'd left home myself, and I never knew what happened to Daniel until I came upon the little show in the Museum of Fine Arts. In the free leaflet I read that he had died in Nanticoke, Maryland, in 1979 and left no survivors.

CHANGELING

"Oraios," *the woman shrieks.* Beautiful. Her hair shoots from her head like wire bristles, the sort of improbable red that can only come out of a bottle, and she's wearing a busily patterned rayon dress. The woman may be well into middle age, but has far from given up. Gold teeth glitter in her jaw. She hefts the sleeping child out of his crib as though he's a sack of onions and, jiggling him, chucks him under the chin. Teddy looks at her with startled pale eyes. "How old?" she asks.

The baby was born in Cambridge, by some lucky chance on the day the first American was launched into space. Lilacs were blooming in their yard when Sandy brought her baby home from the hospital. She feels achingly homesick for their sprawling untidy flat, their friends, the casual student life she then took for granted. "Six months," she answers, holding up five fingers and a thumb. The baby frowns and begins to whimper.

"Ne, ne," the woman says, nodding vigorously. "Big!"

Sandy retrieves her baby from the woman's grasp, lays him on the narrow lumpy bed, and unpins his wet diaper. Meanwhile, the woman has tied a scarf over her hair and, grunting, begins to shove furniture around the living room so she can mop the marble floor underneath it.

One day in September, as Sandy waited to cross the street, her baby in her arms, she saw a long black car drive by with the king and queen inside. Smiling, the queen lifted her hand, and Sandy imagined that the queen bestowed a blessing upon them, a special benison for innocent Americans. That happened days after they arrived, and she and Ed were still staying in the pension near Omonia. Now it's November, and the rainy season has set in.

From the pension they moved to a three-room apartment in Kolonaki, the hilly, rather bleak area to the east of downtown Athens. Ed has gone, with archaeologists and students attached to the American School of Classical Studies, to a dig in the Peloponnesus, near the ancient city of Mycenae. On account of the child, the school forbids her to accompany him. She and the baby are left to fend for themselves.

The maid, Delfinia, will clean the apartment three mornings a week. There isn't much to do in such a small place, but Sandy has been made to understand that giving Delfinia a job is an unwritten condition for renting the place. Since the school arranged the rental—in this country even the simplest transaction seems to involve a web of arcane rules and personal contacts and obligations that are inexplicable to anyone who hasn't lived here for decades—Sandy is stuck with her. The local custom is to provide your cleaning lady with lunch after her four hours of polishing and sweeping and scrubbing. But the household is not big enough for there to be copious leftovers, especially now that Ed is gone, and Sandy finds herself going to the shops and struggling in her terrible Greek to buy powdered soups imported from Holland and similar delicacies to prepare for the woman.

Almost at once Sandy notices that things tend to vanish in Delfinia's wake. Bars of soap, rolls of toilet paper, canned goods, one or two oranges out of the bowl on the kitchen table. In what she hopes is an offhand way Sandy mentions the disappearances to Mrs. Hallick, the wife of the director of ASCS, when she comes to pay a courtesy call. Mrs. H. is large-boned, weathered, her hair bunched in a knot at the back of her head. According to Ed, she's a formidable scholar in her own right, the classifier of thousands of pot shards excavated at the Agora. "Well, my dear, that's simply the way it is here," she replies. "Delfinia is quite likely the principal support of a large family. Children. Grandchildren. Cousins of cousins. Greece is a poor country, you know. You must make allowances."

But Delfinia has teeth made of gold, Sandy thinks. She wears not rags but flowery rayon dresses, even to clean in.

"Some things you have to learn to accept if you want to get along," Mrs. Hallick concludes, setting down her teacup.

She's made Sandy feel both naive and obscenely rich, although her husband's fellowship pays almost nothing for living expenses. In the bedroom Teddy begins to cry, having awakened from his nap. Mrs. Hallick rises and draws on her gloves, eager to return to her classifying, Sandy supposes.

Sandy doesn't care much about the loss of an orange or bar of soap, but the convention of institutionalized theft, however modest the take, makes her uneasy. Delfinia has a key to the place, since she's been the cleaner for previous families connected to ASCS who occupied this apartment, and she expects to let herself in and out. In a way, Sandy feels that she lives here subject to Delfinia's approval or Delfinia's whim.

Back in September, the first time they climbed the hill to the Parthenon, Sandy spotted a clay fragment lying amid rubble. She brushed the dust off with her thumb. "Could this be part of a fertility goddess?" she asked. "Look, surely that's a breast, a hip."

Ed smiled benignly, squinting in the sun. "Could be."

Sandy was lightheaded from the heat and the wine they'd drunk at lunch. She closed her fingers around the warm terracotta and felt, strangely, an intimate connection to it, almost like the joining of lovers, of mother and child. Suddenly she thought she understood something important about Ed's devotion to the classical world. "Past and present are so much bound together here," she said. "It must move you, to know that."

"But they aren't."

Marching onward, Teddy bobbing along in a carrier on his back, Ed began to talk about how the ancient Athenians were swallowed up by the Roman Empire and thereby acquired Christianity, a drearier religion than the one they'd had before, the way you'd catch smallpox or syphilis, and subsequently came the Goths and the Huns and the Slavs and God knows who else, mixing in their blood and wrecking what remained of Attic culture, and finally the Turks, who hung around town for some five hundred years. "Where do you suppose *baklava* came from?" he asked. "And that yogurt you're so fond of? The truth is, there's little if any connection between past and present in Athens. Pericles would never recognize these people."

Ed was probably right, as usual. Sandy adjusted Teddy's hat, which was too big and kept flopping down over his eyes, making him look silly, poor child. Ed looked silly, too, hairy legs sticking gawkily out of baggy shorts, face red in the heat, a blob of suntan lotion on his nose.

"Nothing stays the same," Ed said when they'd trudged uphill for a while. "No matter how much we wish it would sometimes."

"You don't have to tell me that," she replied, annoyed, though she understood he'd only been trying to be kind.

The marble floor is cold on Sandy's bare feet. Another rainy day. She gathers stiff dried diapers from the rack in front of the electric fire and begins to fold them. They smell scorched. Though breakfast is barely over, Teddy is already restless in his playpen and whining to be picked up. Sandy's love for her son is as physical as hunger or a toothache. Still, she wouldn't mind having a moment to herself once in a while.

She doesn't exactly resent her husband. She'd been excited at the prospect of spending two years abroad and proud of Ed's fellowship, encouraging him to accept it. But she does resent ASCS and its absurd Victorian rules. Conditions in the hostel near the dig are unsuitable for children, too "rough," decrees the crotchety widow in charge of student arrangements, and when, at Sandy's urging, Ed appeals the matter to Old Fart Hallick himself, naturally the director sides with the widow. Sandy doesn't buy that excuse for a minute. It's as if getting married when you're an undergraduate, and then having a baby before your husband's career is well established, together amount to sheer irresponsibility, which cannot be allowed to go unpunished.

Sandy wishes, in her meaner moods, that her husband had more backbone, would insist, demand, that his family be with him in Mycenae. Ed doesn't seem to mind being gone for weeks at a time or notice that he has left his wife nearly incommunicado in a country that has only a broken-down mail service and hardly any telephones.

Sandy lifts her baby from his wooden-barred prison and hugs him tightly. "It's just you and me, kid," she says into his brown wispy hair. She tries to find comfort in the warmth and heft of his body, but this has never been a cuddly child, and immediately he's struggling to wrestle himself out of her arms. "What a *busy* baby," Ed's mother said when Teddy was newborn, an irritable infant who would startle at sounds only he could hear, shifts in air current only he could feel, who never seemed content. Now he'd rather investigate the electric fire or stick his finger into an outlet than be held by his mother.

Today, thank God, is not one of Delfinia's days here. Sandy hates the racket of local pop music played at top volume on the woman's transistor radio, the reek of floral perfume that lingers in the apartment long after Delfinia has gone.

The rain lets up a little, and Sandy decides to go for a walk. She zips Teddy into the snowsuit her mother airmailed to her on an emergency basis. Who would have thought it ever got cold in Greece? Who would have imagined that once your parcel reached Athens you'd have to spend hours in a customs shed with men pushing in line ahead of you and then, when you finally got to the counter, ransom your baby's snowsuit for one hundred percent duty? With Teddy in his carrier on her back she negotiates the uneven, stony pavement. The houses in Kolonaki are postwar, middle-class, barren-looking. This is definitely not the Greece of travel posters, revelers in native dress dancing with abandon in *tavernas*. In Kolonaki the women wear sunglasses and clothe their trim figures in knit suits and keep to themselves.

"Why do we have to live way up here?" she asked Ed when she was first shown the place. "Why can't we live downtown where things are happening?"

"You're interested in running water? A fridge? A toilet that isn't a hole in the floor?"

Actually, she'd enjoy the adventure of managing without those things, for a while, anyway, but arguing turned out to be futile. "You wouldn't want Teddy catching some disease, would you?" Once again Ed and the people at the school had ganged up on her.

In the *plateia,* Sandy stops at the butcher's. Skinned carcasses of goats and sheep dangle from hooks in the low ceiling. She buys a quarter kilo of ground beef, in spite of the fact that beef tastes odd here. According to Mrs. Hallick, it's because they don't hang the beef before they hack it up to sell. Sandy has found that the scrawny local chickens barely yield to a day's stewing. The only decent chickens are frozen, from Poland, Mrs. H. says. Sandy will get one for Thanksgiving, when Ed will be home.

At the greengrocer she buys some woody monsters of carrots, and a kilo of potatoes, and a few bananas to mash for Teddy.

Unpacking her groceries in the kitchen, she hears the yogurt-seller's moaning call in the street: *yaourti, yaourti.* He is a gnarled, dark-skinned man who drags his wares behind him in a cart, as if he once had a donkey but the animal died or poverty forced him to sell it. The yogurt, which is made of goat's milk, comes in brown china crocks with circles of paper stuck protectively to the skin. You must wash the crocks and give them back to him when he comes around again, and then while you're standing in the street, exposed, you're morally obliged to buy more.

She leaves Teddy wailing in the playpen and runs into the street carrying the empty dishes. When she drops the coins into his hand, the dark man grins with a vague hint of menace. His teeth are broken and stained. He looks like a gypsy, or an illustration from *Arabian Nights.*

At first she loved the sour, custard-textured yogurt, which was delicious with grainy sugar crystals layered in a thick crust on the surface, but now she's sick of it. She can't persuade Teddy to eat the stuff, either, and Delfinia apparently disdains it, so Sandy ends up flushing the yogurt she buys down the toilet. She has to admit she's a bit afraid of the man, unwilling to cross him by failing to return his crockery and purchase his yogurt.

Ed is back in Athens for four days over Thanksgiving. Sandy has made up her mind not to complain about her isolation and homesickness, since doing so makes her sound like a person without inner resources, and she listens quietly to his accounts of the dig at Mycenae. The spectacular finds were all made in the nineteenth century, the gold masks and crowns, the daggers and jewelry: Sandy has seen these treasures displayed in the Archaeological Museum, on trips she takes with Teddy on her back. Now, at Mycenae, it's a matter of sifting grain by grain through layers of debris in minor tombs, finding nothing of interest to anyone but scholars, as far as she can tell. It's not even clear to Sandy why ASCS is excavating this site, except that Rockefeller or somebody gave them the money to do it. But what does she know, she was an English major.

The expensive Polish chicken is defrosting in the kitchen sink. Ed, leaning against a whitewashed wall, talks about the archaeologists on the dig. One classicist in particular, the brilliant Elinor Warshofski. Sandy remembers her from the Hallicks' cocktail party in September: slim in a figured sundress, crinkled strawberry-blond hair down to her waist, pink eyelids, tenure track at Princeton. Sandy herself hasn't lost all the weight she gained in her pregnancy, and her short nondescript hair is straight, limp in this weather. She doesn't even have a B.A., and her education is on hold, perhaps indefinitely.

"Elinor's instincts are remarkable," Ed says. "Such finely tuned sensibilities, such a subtle mind."

"It's not too rough for her in the hostel?"

"Rough? What are you talking about?" He plucks a grape from a bunch on the drain board and pops it into his mouth.

"Cut that out. They're for the salad."

He works his tongue around the grape to separate pulp from skin and seeds, which he spits into the garbage bag, and helps himself to another.

Elinor thinks this, Elinor speculates that. Is he smitten with her? Sandy wonders, taking a cauliflower out of the tinny little fridge. It won't matter if he is, because Elinor Warshofski is too full of herself to notice the likes of Ed: Ph.D. not yet in hand and one measly article published in a second-rate journal.

Whenever the baby naps they move his crib into the living room and make love hurriedly in the lumpy bed. On Monday her husband is gone again, driving off in their battered VW Camping Bus, leaving behind half a cold chicken in the fridge.

It's at night, after she has put Teddy to bed and washed the supper dishes and perhaps written an air letter to her parents, or worked through a lesson in her *Modern Greek for Beginners* book, that Sandy feels her isolation most acutely. She begins to imagine the electric fire shorting out and setting the apartment ablaze, or a thief breaking the glass in the kitchen window and climbing in, or Teddy suddenly running a high fever. She has no telephone. She would not be able to communicate with her neighbors even if she could penetrate their dark walled houses.

One night as she prepares for bed she notices that her pearl ring, a family piece that Ed's mother gave her the night before the wedding, is missing from the dish on her bureau. Delfinia has taken it, Sandy is certain, picked it out from among the inexpensive earrings and pins, slipped it into the pocket of her apron. Perhaps the woman had no idea of the ring's worth but something about it appealed to her. Perhaps she sold it in the market for a few drachmas or gave it to one of her many grandchildren as a birthday present.

Sandy searches the bedroom and then the entire apartment while Teddy, awakened by the yanking open of drawers, hangs onto the bars of his crib and blubbers. She'll never see the ring again, she knows. When confronted, Delfinia will deny any knowledge of it, and who could prove otherwise? Mrs. Hallick would no doubt take Delfinia's side. *You must have mislaid it, my dear.*

Delfinia probably thinks she's entitled to the ring, or any other small possession of Sandy's she happens to fancy. This is Delfinia's country, her culture; she has to provide for her own. *Some things you have to learn to accept.*

Sandy hardly sleeps that night, blaming herself for being so stupidly trusting. Ed will blame her too, not only for being trusting, but for being careless, as well. She can't do anything right.

Upon arising in the morning Sandy finds the ring on the sill in the bathroom. She has no memory at all of leaving it there, and it occurs to her that Delfinia might have moved it to the sill to set Sandy back on her heels, to give her something to think about.

A few weeks before Christmas Sandy puts Teddy into the back carrier and walks to the *plateia,* where she hires a taxi to take her into town. The air is damp and raw. From a street vendor she buys a waist-high spruce with eight or nine spindly arms and crossed wooden slats nailed to the base of the trunk. Awkwardly hauling the tree, she weaves through the crowds. In the carrier Teddy yaws sharply to the left and then the right, as if trying to knock her off balance, and she has to keep stopping to wipe his nose. His pale eyes blink, watering. He has inherited his father's sensitive skin, his tendency to rashes and eruptions and allergies.

In the open-air market an old woman dressed all in black beckons to Sandy. "Have a look, Madame." She is selling decorations tangled together in a basket. *"Aftos, aftos,"* Sandy says, pointing out strings of gold and silver glass beads, not knowing the words for them. This one. And this one.

She feels her breasts leaking milk. Teddy is starting to whine, but there's no place to feed him here. Now she notices that his woolen cap is gone. He must have pulled it off and let it drop from his fist, and it lies trampled under a thousand feet somewhere in the market or was snatched up and placed on another child's head. She'd never be able to find it even if she tried to retrace her steps through the narrow, serpentine alleyways.

"Okay, baby," she croons. "Let's go home now."

She has spent far too much on the tree; she'll have to lie to her husband if he should ask how much she paid for it. In the taxi it occurs to her that Greece *has* no trees, for goodness sake, all its forests cut down centuries ago to make ships, or for firewood. This poor thing must have been trucked in from Bulgaria or somewhere—no wonder it cost a king's ransom. Like Hansel and Gretel's bread crumbs, a sprinkling of dried needles trails after her from the cab and up the walk and into the apartment.

Even with the strings of beads draped around its branches and its trunk swaddled in a sheet, the tree looks forlorn. Whatever made her think she could manage to create a proper Christmas, Teddy's first, in this godforsaken country?

Two years. Now it seems like a sentence to her.

The next morning when Sandy awakes she's surprised not to hear the persistent whimper that signals Teddy's need to be nursed and changed. She gets out of bed and pulls the shabby velveteen curtains apart along the rod. For once, it isn't raining. From his crib the baby regards her, eyes alert. Immediately she realizes that something is wrong. This is not her child.

Don't be an idiot, she tells herself, how could it not be? But this child's brown hair is a shade or two darker, his forehead a fraction narrower than Teddy's. Even in this dim light she can see that his eyes are not blue, but gray.

She lifts him out of the crib. He doesn't have Teddy's solid weight. She lays him on the bed and unsnaps his cotton nightgown—yes, that, at least, is the same. The child seems to be studying her, as if wondering who she might be, but displays no fear of her. His skin is what absolutely convinces her that this is not her baby. It's not dark—you couldn't say that—but not pale, either. No diaper rash, no irritation in the folds of the neck, no reddish marks from the impression of a fingernail or diaper pin. His skin is utterly smooth, smooth as the shell of an egg.

Sandy is a famously light sleeper. It would not be possible to enter the room and exchange this child for hers without disturbing her. And yet the incontrovertible fact is that someone has done so.

Doing her best to control her panic, she bundles the child into Teddy's snowsuit and carries him out into the street. Her watch reads shortly past six. Here in Kolonaki, up in the penumbra of Mount Lykabettos, houses are silent and the street empty. Even the maids and handymen aren't up yet. There's a police station in the *plateia;* Ed went there to get some kind of document stamped when they moved into their apartment, and she waited in the VW.

The florist, the pastry shop, the butcher, the greengrocer, the pharmacy are still closed, their corrugated metal shutters yanked down tight over the storefronts and secured with padlocks. The baby is quiet in her arms as she runs.

She hurries up the steps of the police station and through the metal door. Inside is a smell of dust and cigarette smoke and bad plumbing. A man with a shaggy mustache and rumpled uniform sits behind a desk.

"This isn't my baby," she tells him. "Someone took my baby in the night, while I slept, and left this one instead."

It's obvious from his weary, baffled expression that he has not comprehended a single word. He picks up the telephone and says something into it. After a very long time, another policeman appears, this one without a mustache, and she repeats her story.

She realizes how incredibly absurd the story must sound. Crazy American, he has to be thinking. Only one of many crazy Americans who come to Greece and demand that attention be paid to their lunatic notions. Nevertheless, the policeman listens politely until she has finished. He translates for the mustachioed policeman, and then the two of them confer in their language, both of them gesturing with their hands. It's not clear to her whether they believe her tale or not.

Has she, in fact, lost her mind? Sandy asks herself.

Her breasts are sore, inflated with milk. From the crib the baby looks at her expectantly, his gray eyes fixed on her face. She thinks about Teddy hustled away by some stranger, frightened, hungry. She lifts the child out of the crib. She carries him into the living room and sits with him in one of the landlord's heavy mismatched chairs. The baby's head fits perfectly into the crook of her arm. To comfort him, or maybe herself, she begins to sing, the way she sang to Teddy. Tuneless nonsensical words, words summoned unconsciously from her own childhood. *The king is in his counting-house, counting out his money . . . the queen is in the parlor, eating bread and honey . . .* She unbuttons the front of her shirt. Her milk isn't going to let down for this cuckoo in her nest, she is sure, but he takes her nipple whole into his mouth as though it belongs to him. *The maid is in the garden . . .* Intently the child suckles, his small hand on her breast, laying claim to her . . . *hanging out the clothes. Al-o-ong comes a bla-ackbird . . .* Sandy feels the pressure release. Tears run down her cheeks.

Why is this happening to her?

Ed, summoned back from the Peloponnesus, admits that the boy's eyes are darker than he remembered. "But eyes do that, don't they? Darken as the child grows older?"

"How can you not know this isn't your son?" she cries. "How can you be so oblivious?"

"Be reasonable, Sandy. Who would deliberately exchange one child for another? Next you're going to tell me the faeries did it."

Detectives come to the house and dust for fingerprints. The police interview Delfinia and Mrs. Hallick, as well as the merchants in the *plateia* whose shops Sandy frequented and several of the nearby neighbors.

No unusual fingerprints are identified. Delfinia and Mrs. Hallick and the shopkeepers all deny that this baby is not Teddy, or else they confess that they can't be certain, one way or the other. "I'll be honest with you," the butcher says. "Babies, they all look the same to me." The neighbors heard and saw nothing out of the ordinary the night of the alleged exchange. No reports of mysterious blue-eyed and fair-skinned babies appearing in Greek households are received by the authorities.

"Ed," she pleads, "you have to help me. I swear this isn't our baby."

"Look, Sandy, I know you're upset," he replies, softening pink wax earplugs between his fingers, "but you're letting your imagination run away with you. You need a hobby. Why don't you take up painting or something?" He stuffs the plugs into his ears to block out street noises so that, a German dictionary at his elbow, he can concentrate on a monograph lent to him by the Old Fart. The archaeologists have now abandoned the dig for the Christmas season, and Ed will not return to Mycenae until the new year.

When Sandy nurses the baby, he focuses his gray eyes on her face, as though imprinting her image in his brain.

Delfinia comes to the apartment on her usual days, and secretly Sandy keeps watch on her, vigilant for clues. Bustling about the apartment with her brassy hair under a scarf, Delfinia pays no more and no less attention to this baby than she did to Teddy. But then, she'd be careful not to betray herself, wouldn't she, if she were the thief. She isn't stupid. Perhaps this is a grandson for whom she has arranged a better life than the one he was destined for.

Without telling Ed, Sandy goes to the police station in the *plateia* and makes them listen to her suspicions about Delfinia. The policeman who speaks English thinks her idea over. Then he asks, "Who would give up a grandson, bonded by blood, for such a reason? Not even a maid, no. Not in this country." Nevertheless, Sandy insists that he look into the matter, and he promises he will do so. "*Ne, ne. Sigoura.*" Certainly. Of course. But nothing comes of it.

"The yogurt-seller," Sandy says to the policeman on another day. "I always wondered about him, the way he looked at me, as if he might be up to something." "Up to what sort of something?" the policeman asks. "I don't know, some intrigue." The policeman smiles. Yes, he will absolutely investigate this possibility. However, the old man has ceased to ply his trade in her neighborhood, and the police are unable to locate him. Sandy suspects they did not look very hard, if at all. Three brown crocks sit on her kitchen shelf, unredeemed.

Doing dishes after a meal, she suddenly remembers Teddy's birth certificate. It has his little footprint on it; comparing footprints would be a way to persuade everyone she's not hallucinating. Before she and Ed departed for Greece they stowed the birth certificate and other important papers in a safe-deposit box in Porter Square, leaving the keys with Ed's mother out in Weston. Her hands dripping soapy water, Sandy rushes into the living room, where Ed is poring over notes he brought back from the dig. "You've got to go to the school right now," she says. "Use their phone to call your mom. Get her to open the safe-deposit box and send us Teddy's birth certificate."

Ed removes an earplug and stares at her over the rims of his reading glasses. "In the first place," he says, "my mother couldn't legally open the box unless you and I both died."

"But there must be some way, if we notified the bank or the police—"

"And even if she could open it," he continues, "I wouldn't think of asking her to go on this fool's errand. I've been patient so far, but I really don't want to hear any more about this nonsense, all right?"

The next morning, while Ed is researching something in the ASCS library, Sandy takes the changeling to the American Embassy on Vasilissis Sophias, which is not far from Kolonaki. After an hour's wait, she is granted an audience with a vice consul or maybe he's a vice-vice consul, a balding man in a drip-dry suit the color of a tank. Sandy shows him Teddy's passport photo, taken in Cambridge when the child was two months old. Teddy's eyes are like raisins in a rice pudding; the photo must have been overexposed to make them appear so dark. The vice consul looks up at the baby who is dancing on tiptoes in her lap, grinning, clutching a fistful of her shirt. "This child is older," he says stupidly.

"But what I'm trying to tell you is . . ." Explaining the situation to him a second time, she hears her voice, shrill, frustrated, a hint of lunacy in it recognizable even to her.

He taps his ballpoint pen on his blotter. "Does your husband feel the same way you do?"

"Well not exactly, but he never paid that much attention to Teddy in the first place. You see—"

The vice consul advises her that without evidence, without proof, there's nothing he can do. Obviously he assumes she is suffering from some kind of delusion, a form of hysteria he has not before encountered and that he hopes won't be catching—not in his bailiwick.

The day after Ed returns to Mycenae, Sandy straps the changeling into Teddy's back carrier and sets out from the apartment in Kolonaki. A child cannot be secreted forever, she tells herself. Sooner or later she will find her son, even if she has to scour every inch of Athens without help from anyone. In her purse she carries passports, hers and Teddy's, and their return airplane tickets, so that she can make a quick getaway when she finds him. She has only the vaguest idea of what she'll do with the changeling at the moment of discovery. Not simply thrust him into the arms of some passerby as she's hailing a cab, nothing as cruel as that. She'll think of something when the time comes.

Every day she takes a different route, covers a different section of the city, and doesn't return to Kolonaki until she's exhausted. The days lengthen and the weather becomes warmer. By now Sandy has studied the faces of hundreds of babies, peered into shawls and under the awnings of strollers and the hoods of carriages, raised the suspicions of mothers and grandmothers and big sisters and maids, who are perhaps wary of the evil eye. So far no luck, but Sandy doesn't allow herself to give up hope. She's glad that Ed is preoccupied and so far away he can't interfere with her search or scoff at it.

She's sleeping badly and eating only cold food at odd hours, standing in front of the open refrigerator, so that her clothes begin to hang on her. Her hair grows shaggy but she doesn't cut it. She feels in her bones that if she changes anything about herself, does anything for herself, she will destroy the possibility of finding her boy.

Today a disk of sun glows feebly through mist. It's April. The gray-eyed child is humming a little, gently kicking his feet in rhythm with her pace. He has plumped out, first expanding into Teddy's nighties and romper suits and now straining their seams. She feels his weight solidly on her back.

Passing a bakery late in the morning, she decides to buy a loaf of bread, since she left the apartment without bothering to eat breakfast. A dozen or more women are crowded into the shop, jostling one another, shouting in a disorderly way. Finally Sandy manages to catch a shop girl's attention and exchanges some paper money for a coarse yellowish loaf and a few coins. Knowing she has been overcharged, but too weary to complain, Sandy tucks the bread into her string bag. She's hot in the press of people, close to fainting.

Outside, ahead of her on the street, she sees a woman pushing an old-fashioned black perambulator, the kind with huge wheels. In the buggy sits a pale-skinned child, ten or eleven months old. There's no doubt in Sandy's mind that the child is Teddy; she has found him at last. The bread banging into her leg and the carrier thumping against her spine, she runs after the buggy. "Teddy!" she cries, "Teddy!" The woman stops and looks behind her.

There's a sharp pain below Sandy's breastbone. Her breath is ragged as she closes in on the buggy. "Teddy," she says, softly now, to the blank-faced baby. He is ensconced like a prince in embroidered bedding, dressed in a sky-blue knit outfit and matching cap that Sandy has never seen before. This is certainly her baby, and yet he seems so thin. Insubstantial. Before the woman understands what's happening, Sandy plucks the cap from Teddy's head, so that she can examine his hair. "*Ochi, ochi,*" the woman gasps. The hair is brown, yes, but so dark—is it only that it's longer and thicker now? And it curls at the nape of the neck. Would Teddy's have done that?

All of a sudden Sandy's not sure whether this is her child or not. How *can* she be sure, after so many weeks, months, have passed? Showing no recognition at all, the child turns his head away. The woman grabs the cap out of Sandy's hand. A man takes her by the arm and says something along the lines of *What's your problem, lady?* The woman moves briskly onward over the cobblestones, buggy wheels squealing.

After a while Sandy finds herself on the street where she saw the king and queen drive by, way back in September. No limousine today, no gracious wave of a hand. Sandy sits on a marble step in front of some kind of official building and releases the baby from the carrier. She pulls the loaf out of the bag, tears off the heel for him. Happily he gnaws his bread and she eats some herself. With the hem of her shirt she wipes soggy crumbs from his chin. "Okay, baby," she says, "let's go home."

DYSLEXIA

When I left home for the first time I did what everyone dreamed of doing back in 1959: I went to live in Greenwich Village. It wasn't like what you think, though. I boarded with my pregnant second cousin Lorrie Mickle, and helped take care of her little kid, and commuted uptown to a precariously financed Catholic college for women. What I learned about life that year was mostly secondhand. Even so, I was often glad that Ma, up in Somerville, Mass., didn't know any more than that I was living with a respectable Italian family in a wholesome Catholic atmosphere.

Lorrie was Italian, all right, but you'd never have guessed it from the way she looked. Her hair was light brown, fine and straight, and her eyes such a pale blue that you could see the structure of the iris, like loops of wire set in glass. Her elbows were scaly, as though constantly irritated by clothing and sheets. She followed lists; her whole day was governed by them. Lists tacked inside cupboards, taped to refrigerator shelves, dangling from light cords. "John types them out for me," she explained. "But then if it's too complicated, I can't follow the list," she said, sighing. "They wonder where I sprouted from, the only one in the family with dyslexia. A changeling? A little hanky-panky on the part of my mother?"

We talked in the kitchen, at the back end of the flat. The one window was barred so that burglars couldn't get in from the fire escape. "Well, if you knew my mother," Lorrie went on, "you'd rule that out, at least. My mother is a very moral person. One time John and I pinched some corn from a farmer's field over in Jersey, and she wouldn't eat it because it was stolen goods. It turned out to be horse corn and *nobody* could eat it. She said that's what happens to evil-doers, they get their just reward."

Evie Mickle leaned over the side of her highchair and threw bits of hot dog down to Albert, the cat.

"Do you think that's true, Chris? Personally, I doubt it." Lorrie's eyeglasses were steamed from the pot in which broccoli was boiling. "Or at least retribution happens such a long time after the evil act that the victim doesn't give a damn anymore. Unless the victim happens to be the type who holds a grudge, but I'm not like that, are you?"

She wiped Evie's round pale little face with the end of a dish towel. "For instance, when John's mother refused to come to our wedding I hoped she'd fall off a roof or something, but now I don't care anymore. So if something *did* happen to her it wouldn't break my heart, but I wouldn't think God struck her down because of something she did to me. You know?"

Lorrie made martinis, as well as everything else, by the list method. She and John drank what seemed to me then an extraordinary amount. I was reading Hardy for my English lit class and so, unlike Lorrie, I felt that fate and retribution hung heavily over people. Yet the Mickles' lives, in spite of lists, seemed completely unfocused. Events had no beginnings or resolutions that I could discern.

I drank my first martini listening to Lorrie's account of their courtship, which had something to do with a bowl of chocolate mousse she'd been carrying on the Eighth Avenue subway, but the essence of their relationship eluded me. It wasn't only the gin causing my confusion. How *had* this vague, breathless daughter of an obscure New Jersey Italian family managed to connect with a portly graduate of Yale Law School? There must have been more to it than a mousse, but sequential analysis wasn't Lorrie's strong point.

Their apartment was on West 11th Street, four flights up, a long set of rooms connected like a train. Dark, cockroach-infested, and rent-controlled, but with a certain amount of charm, mostly due to

Lorrie's influence, and that inadvertent. A cocktail guest gave Evie a beanbag in the form of a beaver, and Lorrie absentmindedly draped it over the back of a chair. Nobody moved it; the beaver became part of the ambience, its toothy ironic expression silently commenting on John's pronouncements. She'd buy things in neighborhood shops on impulse: a steel engraving of Stonehenge, a roll-top desk with legs like pasta twists. Shabby the apartment was, but not Ma's kind of shabby, no splintering veneer or brocade upholstery, worn and faintly soiled like too-long trousers. Every object at the Mickles' was unashamedly itself, and that enchanted me.

My room opened off the living room, separated by a sliding door. The parquet floor buckled and the ceiling was so high compared to the size of the room that it was like living in an elevator shaft. In my little room I discovered Burckhardt and Burke, Skelton, Yeats, Huizinga, Bosch. Because of her reading disability Lorrie's education was spottier even than mine; she picked up snatches of information in the same eclectic way she collected furniture. Late at night we sat on my bed looking at reproductions of *The Garden of Earthly Delights.*

"There are no children in this garden," she remarked, puzzled. "Plenty of sex, but no children." In my paper I elaborated on her observation—the sterility of lust in the symbolic imagery of Hieronymus Bosch—and my art history teacher wrote in the margin, "Good insight!"

If Lorrie gave me insights about Bosch she offered few about her husband, or at least what their marriage was all about. John Mickle worked in the legal department of a Wall Street bank; he was a massively built man with the same bland, pale face as his daughter. He had a former wife living on East 70th Street, two teenaged children, and vast debts. Not only was he paying alimony and child support, but he was sending the son to a boarding school in Connecticut and the daughter to a psychiatrist. All this explained the poverty in which he and Lorrie lived. Selective poverty, though. They always had money for gin, whatever threats came from exasperated creditors.

There were threats of another kind, too. Now and then the first wife, Sally, would call up and tell Lorrie that she was about to commit suicide because of what Lorrie and John had done to her. "John left her because she's a lunatic, but he can't escape her, you know? And his mother eggs her on. They're all from Minneapolis," Lorrie explained obscurely. "Once Sally actually did cut her wrists with a razor, so we have to take her seriously. John goes flying around to her apartment, and she gives him this long harangue, and then he comes home and gets drunk. He goes to work looking like a death's-head, or else he doesn't go at all. She'll probably get him fired, which will be killing the goose that lays the golden egg, but she's too hysterical to realize it. I may not know right from left, but at least I know that."

"What made you and John decide to get married?"

She smoothed the T-shirt over her big belly and pondered. "John wanted to impose some order on my life, and it seemed like a sensible idea at the time."

"Was your life *more* disordered before?"

"Oh"—she wiggled her fingers vaguely—"I used to have affairs a lot. I was in love with this Indian—he was a Micmac—but he was already married. I had to have an abortion, and of course my mother wasn't exactly wild about all that, so when John came along she was relieved, even though he's divorced and a Protestant. At least he works on Wall Street." She laughed. "My Micmac didn't work at all."

In the spring term all my classes met in the morning. I'd study until three or so in my room and then take Evie to a little park on Bleecker Street. As unlike to her mother as Lorrie must have been, so Evie was to Lorrie. A whole family of changelings, I thought. Lorrie talked all the time; Evie didn't talk at all, although she was two and a half, an age at which nearly all children have at least mastered "no." One of the mothers in the park asked me if Evie was a foreign child, *un*learning some language before picking up English. Speech or no, Evie communicated without trouble. Her grip (on toys) was like Elmer's, and she bit when provoked.

John worried that Evie's hearing might be impaired, and he made an appointment for Lorrie to take her to an ENT man uptown. The verdict was that her hearing and intelligence were normal; she'd talk when she found something important enough to say.

Late one afternoon when we were returning from the park, Evie happened to look up and see Albert the cat staring out the apartment window. "He wants to get out," she said matter-of-factly, more to herself than to me.

I rang the bell about fifty-seven times and when the lock was released from upstairs I shouted up the stairwell, "Lorrie!"

"What's the matter," she cried.

"Evie just said a five-word sentence." Several doors on the intervening floors opened and shut.

"What did she say?"

I was struggling up the stairs with Evie in one arm, dragging the stroller behind me. Lorrie met me half way.

"She said, 'He wants to get out.'"

"Who?"

"Albert. She saw him in the window looking down on West 11th Street."

"Oh God," Lorrie said, striking her forehead with the palm of her hand.

She was getting very pregnant, only a month to go, she thought, though John was skeptical of her calculations. She'd never bought maternity clothes when she was expecting Evie and couldn't see any reason to do so this time around, either. Mostly she wore T-shirts stretched over jeans which were left unzipped and tied together from button to hole with a shoelace. But on the day she was to go to a fundraising luncheon at my college, Sacred Heart, she dressed in a pink Mexican smock with phoenixes and camellias embroidered on it.

We sat in the kitchen drinking red vermouth on ice cubes before she left. She had to steel herself for the occasion, especially since the subway trip involved two changes and there was always the possibility she'd end up in Flushing Meadow.

"What *is* the influence you have at Sacred Heart?" I asked her. "How were you able to get me a scholarship?"

"Oh Chris, it's not me, it's John. One of his friends at the bank is a trustee. When I got pregnant again John cooked up this plan of getting one of my relatives to help me with Evie, because he doesn't really trust me. Turned out, though, you could have walked into the place without any help from me or John or any trustee." She blinked at me sadly behind her glasses. "The truth is you should have gone some place better, Marymount, or Barnard, even. You have brains, not like me."

"Lorrie, you have brains. Why do you let people belittle you?"

"What people?"

"John is the example that leaps to mind."

"Oh no. I'd get into terrible messes if he weren't around to tell me what to do."

"Seems to me he messed up his own life pretty well before he met you. Lunatic wife, two obnoxious children."

"That wasn't his fault," she said, taking Evie onto her lap.

"He married her."

Lorrie laughed a little. "She was pregnant."

"You see."

"But you never know, do you, how a marriage is going to work out over the long haul? Even if Sally hadn't been pregnant. You love somebody and then . . ." She looked around her in a muddled sort of way, as though surprised to find herself in this dark, barred kitchen, decorated with grease-specked lists and mousetraps under the sink. "Marriage is really like a junk heap, things falling down on the things that have gone before. And then it all gets packed together and turns into something hard, like coal. But you can't see any order to it. Unless there's a divorce, and then everybody digs it all up again—the counselors, the shrinks, the lawyers—and then there's even less order." She kissed the back of Evie's neck in an abstracted way. Her breath ruffled Evie's hair, which was as pale as a dandelion gone to seed. "Better to let it lie there," she said, sighing.

"Turning into diamonds."

"Coal to diamonds. Yeah, well. Oh, Chris, how she's wrinkled me," she said, looking at the Mexican dress when Evie slipped from her lap to run after Albert. "Let's hope they'll fall out in the subway."

In March John's brother Oliver arrived, unbidden, from Minneapolis. He was the baby of the family. After graduating from the University of Minnesota with a less than distinguished record, he had been selling vacuum cleaners door-to-door, unsuccessfully. He slept on the sofa and in a random way looked for work. His presence exasperated John in ways I could only guess at; apparently years of carrot-and-stick approaches to his behavior had ended only in stalemate. Oliver seemed oblivious to John's crankiness. Lorrie tended to side with Oliver, or at least to give him aid and comfort. During the day, while John was at work and Oliver was supposedly looking for work, they sat in the kitchen for long hours, Oliver complaining cheerfully about how the world conspired against him.

Oliver had John's broad face, but not his bulk. The most charming thing about him was his hair, which was longer than the fashion then—probably because he was too lazy to get it cut—and was brown and soft, falling across his forehead in an engaging way. Clearly, he was attracted to me from the beginning. There was a strange moment when, in the middle of some conversation and for a reason I can no longer remember, Lorrie said, "Chris is beautiful," and Oliver quickly said, "Of course," as though Lorrie had said, "Albert is a cat," or, "The ceiling has cracks in it."

Oliver found a job, or to be more exact, John relented and finagled a job for him at the bank, as some sort of minor functionary in the mortgage department. Oliver took me out to a Greek restaurant to celebrate, having borrowed the money from Lorrie. We drank retsina, an experience new to us both. "Distilled charcoal," Oliver said, laughing. "It's a long way from Minneapolis."

"A long way from Somerville, too."

"No Greeks there?"

"Oh yes, there are Greeks. What I meant was that there are so many things in New York I'd never heard of before."

"Like?"

"Dyslexia," saying the first thing that came into my head.

"Let's see, that would be a . . . maladjustment to lawyers," Oliver offered.

"Good try." I laughed, remembering my high school Latin, and thinking that Oliver undoubtedly had his brother and himself in mind. "It's actually the word for Lorrie's disability, her confusion over words and time and order."

"I didn't know it was a disease. I thought it was a virtue."

"Well, I suppose that depends on what society you live in. Maybe in sixteenth-century Flanders no one would have noticed."

"Why then?"

"I was thinking of Bosch. Whatever order there is in his paintings isn't our kind of order."

"No," he said, with a certain amount of melancholy. "Especially the order at the Bankers Distrust."

"You'll do all right, Oliver."

We had stewed figs with cream for dessert, very rich and sweet. We walked back to 11th Street with our arms around each other. It was after midnight when we got home, and the apartment was dark. "Can I come and lie with you in your room?" Oliver whispered to me.

"Oh, Oliver. I'm not ready yet."

"All right," he said gently. "Patience is my middle name."

Within a week Oliver was fired and sent back to his mother in Minneapolis. No one ever explained to me what his transgression was, though there seemed to be some kind of disgrace attached; the sin was more than incompetence. John stalked the apartment in a rage while Oliver packed. A taxi was sent for. Lorrie wept and Evie careened around the furniture and up and down the length of the hallway on her kiddie-cart. There was no chance for a private word. He never wrote to me; probably it was more than he could manage to lay hands on paper, pen, and postage simultaneously.

The strange thing was that at seven in the morning the day after Oliver left, a Sunday, the entire ceiling in the living room fell to the floor. If Oliver had been sleeping there, he might have been killed.

John viewed the devastation, mixed himself a martini, and went back to bed.

That's how it was at the Mickles'. If the ceiling wasn't falling in, John's other wife was threatening suicide or wheat bugs were discovered in the Cheerios. But soon after Oliver left something happened that upset Lorrie more than anything else. Evie opened a window in the living room and Albert, seizing the opportunity, leapt from the sill to the sidewalk, four flights down.

I came home from class to find Lorrie in the kitchen, dazedly washing a pile of dishes. The cat was on the table, stiff already, with dried blood around his mouth and ears.

"Evie said he wanted to get out," Lorrie said, "and she was right."

"Albert left," Evie observed, looking with casual interest at the corpse on the table.

"What are we going to do with him? We don't even have a garden to bury him in," Lorrie said, tears beginning to drip into the dish water.

"I'll take care of it," I told her. I wrapped Albert in newspaper and stuffed the mummified body into a shopping bag. I walked along West 11th Street and around the corner to Waverly Place. Images from the film *Rear Window* sprang into mind; I imagined myself being arrested for murder or, at the very least, unlawful disposal of a dead animal. Outside the service entrance of a restaurant I came upon a dumpster on wheels. Trying to look as inconspicuous as possible, I shoved Albert in among the orange halves and pork chop bones and clamped the lid on tight.

Lorrie had put Evie down for her nap, and she came and sat on the edge of my bed while I unpacked my textbooks.

"I made the sign of the cross over him," I said, hoping to comfort her, but my words had the opposite effect.

"I loved that damn cat," she said.

"I know."

"Evie knew all the time what was in Albert's head. Sometimes I think there's something odd about that child, the way she stares. Like she has second sight."

"Perceptive, that's called."

"It's unnatural," she said, scaring herself with the thought. "Supposing I'm giving birth to monsters. Supposing my mother was right, and this is my reward for a bad life."

She lay on the bed, her belly hugely distended, and I came and sat next to her. "You're the nicest person I know," I said. Evie would have a way to go before she could figure out what was in her mother's head, I thought fondly. She took my hand and placed it on her belly. I felt little bulges, elbows and knees and feet, shoving against her skin, like a cat under a blanket.

"That feels so nice, your warm hand," she said, closing her eyes. After a while she slept.

The baby was born at 2:30 the next morning. It was a boy, a perfectly normal infant, and they named him Thomas.

THE COCOANUT GROVE

He is lying on his stomach. I can see out of the corner of my eye that his shoes are on the oatmeal wool upholstery. The boy has a soft body, the unused musculature of the mentally ill. The smell all around him is of men's cologne, the kind somebody might buy in a drugstore for a last-minute gift.

"This place always so slow?" he asks me. His voice drags, and it's muffled in the couch.

"Most of the doctors are on vacation in August."

"The library's only for doctors?"

"The doctors, and the other members of the staff."

"No patients."

"No."

This information doesn't seem to bother him; in fact, he goes to sleep.

I am sitting at a table, checking one tray of catalog cards against another. The first tray represents the Greenspan Collection, which I am accessioning; the second tray represents the library's collection. I am eliminating duplicates, "dupes" we call them in the library profession. Already I have arranged the Greenspan books—nearly five hundred of them—alphabetically by main entry along the shelf formed by the climate control system. Cooled air stirs dust up from the bindings. It's not an ideal arrangement from a book-preservation point of view, but it doesn't much matter, since these books have been ignored and abused for years. Besides, most of them date from the fifties and tend to be sociological rather than medical, so that now, a quarter of a century later, Ruth more or less scorns them.

After a while the boy turns over and tries to strike a match, but he can't get it to light. "How much this building cost, anyway?"

"I don't know."

He lies there, contemplating.

"Is that a doctor in there, talking to her?"

"Her" is Ruth, the librarian. We can hear voices coming from her office, and they are arguing, but it's hard to tell whether the argument is personal or professional in nature.

"Probably."

"How many doctors in this place?"

"I don't know that, either. I don't really work here. I'm a volunteer."

"You mean you're working and not getting paid for it?" He is incredulous. "That's shit. You got to make enough money to take care of yourself."

"I have enough money."

"You a housewife?"

"Well, I'm married. But I don't spend much time cleaning my house."

The conversation lapses, and I'm hoping he'll get bored with me and go away. I don't like being cross-examined and I don't like his smell.

Then he asks, "*You* ever write a book?"

Reluctantly I tell him. "I wrote a novel once. It was never published, though."

"Did it have violence in it?"

I have to think back. "No, not really."

"You got a match?"

I pick up my handbag and root around in there. I can feel him watching me. His shirt is wet all around the armpits and he looks unshaven, although he's probably no more than sixteen or seventeen. But big, coarsely dark, with a pale face. On the floor by the couch is an Algebra II book with a broken spine, papers spilling out of it. I toss him the matchbook.

His cigarettes are as battered as the algebra book; he lights the frayed end of one. "You want it?"

"No, thanks." I smile, to compensate for refusing and for disliking him.

"That's why you didn't get it published."

"What?"

"No violence in your novel."

I'm not sure whether he's being ironic. But I can see him turning over that idea in his head: violent acts that I might commit to paper. Yet he seems too listless to care much. The cigarette burns down on the glass top.

I turn back to my card trays, and after some time he gets up and wanders away, leaving the algebra book on the floor.

Working in the mental health center is in some ways unsettling. The building is new, constructed and supported by the state, on the site of a former slum. It's made of poured concrete, molded into vertical corrugations both inside and out. There are no square corners; even the toilets have curved walls. The windows are curtained with narrow vertical slats and the light is artificial.

It's now mid-morning, and I'm taking a break in Ruth's office. At the moment she is putting together a bibliography on the Cocoanut Grove fire for one of the staff doctors. This doctor has a patient, a college girl, who is the survivor of a dormitory fire in Providence. Because she hasn't been responding to psychiatric treatment, the doctor wants to study case histories of other fire victims.

Ruth's office is mercifully free of corrugations, and she has dozens of museum postcards taped to the walls. There is also a handwritten sign saying, *Plus ça change, plus c'est la même chose.* For some reason the architect has supplied this small office with an industrial-size stainless steel sink; on the counter beside it is a bowl of nectarines and a toothbrush. The bookcase holds *Das Kapital* and a volume of Oscar Wilde's essays, as well as various books on mental illness that are waiting to be shelved. Under her desk are a pair of sandals and a pair of clogs, but Ruth's feet are bare.

She is typing. Over her shoulder I read, "Search of *Index Medicus* under subject heading 'fire' yielded nil."

"We'll have to branch out into other disasters," she says to me. "Polio victims, survivors of war. Generalized survivors' neuroses." She shrugs and smiles. She is wearing a blue cotton sundress. I can detect the beginnings of a double chin, and her neck has concentric creases, although she's not yet thirty and not overweight. She wears no rings or other jewelry.

"I once knew a nurse," I tell her, "who was on duty at Boston City when they began to bring in the Cocoanut Grove survivors. She didn't leave the hospital for three days." The nurse was my first husband's mother, but I decide not to open up that subject.

"Yeah." Ruth has a way of looking carefully at you when she's talking to you; she doesn't fiddle with a pencil or pull at her hair. Her attentiveness is almost like a therapeutic technique. "Yeah, but a crisis gives you strength at the time. It's afterward you get the problem."

She locates some journal citations and when she goes to the periodical room I tag along, because Greenspan's collection contains a number of odd back issues of journals that eventually I will have to deal with.

"There's no money for binding," she says. "Or anything else, for that matter."

"I'm surprised you let the unbound issues circulate."

"If I don't, the doctors steal them instead."

In fact, the whole health center has the air of being casually and constantly ripped off. Kids from the North Station neighborhood wander through, looking for something to lift. And possibly the building itself (no corners, no smooth surfaces) makes even psychiatrists lose touch with ordinary proprieties.

"But," Ruth goes on, "I may change my mind about circulating periodicals. I have trouble making decisions and sticking to them," she admits with a sigh. "That's true in my life . . . and here, too."

Outside the periodical room there are stains on the carpet, as though somebody once entered the library with something black on his left foot.

An hour later, the boy is back, lying on the couch and smoking. A woman with oversized blue-tinted eyeglasses and an irritable manner appears. She is the Director of Social Services, down from upstairs.

"Did she call the police on you?" she shouts to the boy.

"No. Why should she?"

"Why shouldn't she?"

"I'm not doing anything," he says calmly.

It's strange that they call Ruth "she" and not by name, but it must be Ruth they are referring to. The social services woman leaves, stymied for the moment.

Again, the boy and I can hear voices in Ruth's office. It's a man, one of the doctors. He walks into the library and looks at the boy; his face seems pinched, as though the expression is held in place with clothespins. I recognize him to be Dr. Cady, for whom Ruth is preparing the Cocoanut Grove bibliography.

"Is that your algebra book?" he asks, in a threatening way.

"Algebra is one of the things I'm good at."

"Let's go. Upstairs."

As he passes me, the boys says matter-of-factly, "He fucks her. She goes up to his office and he fucks her."

He leaves a can of Coke, unopened, sweating on the glass-topped table.

I'm in the stacks, checking whether the duplicates I've identified in the card tray are actually on the shelves. Ruth comes to the end of the row and says, "Well, that's one thing about working in the bin."

"What?"

"He put his hand down my dress."

I don't know whether she means the boy or Dr. Cady, and I don't know whether I'm supposed to look distressed or not; probably it betrays civilian status to look distressed.

"He came into the office and asked whether Stelazine makes you fat, and that's a legitimate reference question—right? So I got out the *PDR* and made a show of looking it up, and I told him no, and then he put his hand down the front of my dress.

"And then he backed off, really upset, and I told him it's okay. It's okay, only don't do it again.

"It wasn't me who told Dr. Cady. He turned himself in. He was looking for limits." Her neck is flushed. She doesn't seem embarrassed, but she's not quite in control of the situation, either.

"I'm going out for lunch. If he comes back, call upstairs at this number. Dr. Cady says he's not allowed in the library now." She writes on a scrap of yellow paper. "No, wait a minute. Here's the number for building security. Call them, that's faster."

"What's the boy's name?"

She hesitates a moment. "I don't know his name. If I ever knew it, I don't remember. Just say it's a large male patient who's not supposed to be in the library. Dr. Cady's orders."

"He left a Coke on the table," I say, feeling somewhat foolish.

"Oh, that was a peace offering for me," she says, smiling. "You can drink it if you want."

LEVITATION

Molly stood on the linoleum in her bare feet. She closed her eyes and stretched her arms sideways. The muscles in her upper back tightened. She ignored the grit under her feet and turned her palms upward, concentrating on a mental picture of the peak above her head, where two sharply angled panels of sheetrock joined. "Rise," she whispered. "Rise."

With the heel of her boot Diane shoved shut the door behind her. "Hi," she said, out of breath from climbing up two flights. Stooping to avoid cracking her skull, she set the grocery bag on the strip of buckled countertop crammed between sink and wall. Inside were a couple of boxes of macaroni and cheese dinner, a carton of milk, some golden delicious apples, and a head of lettuce. She didn't unpack them, partly because she didn't want to intrude on her daughter's space and partly because she cringed at the thought of what might lie behind the cupboard and refrigerator doors. "What are you doing?" she asked.

"Levitating," Molly said.

Diane's eyes fell on Molly's feet. Rather stumpy feet, if truth be told, with high insteps like her father's. A puckered seam on the right one where she'd had an operation for osteomyelitis when she was in fourth grade. "You don't seem to have got very far," she observed.

"I was interrupted." Molly opened her eyes and watched her mother shucking her boots. Her hair had grown out some from its last perm and had an aura, a suggestion, of gray about it that made Molly

40

think of old snow thinly dusted with new. "Thanks for the grub," Molly said, "but I'm not destitute, you know. I do have a job."

Diane eased a section of newspaper out from the garbage can and set her boots on it next to the door. "I'm not sure I think of working half-time in a copy center as a *job,* exactly," she said. Molly, silent, either meditating or biting her tongue, sat down on a rag rug. Diane believed she recognized that rug. Molly must have liberated it from its Limbo in the basement at home. As Diane began to unbutton her coat she heard something—rustling, like somebody wrapping Christmas presents in secret. "What's that?" she asked.

Molly clasped her ankles. Slowly she curled her spine so her forehead touched her feet. "What's what?"

"That noise. It's not rats, is it?"

Equally slowly Molly uncurled. "Red squirrels," she said. "They make nests in the insulation."

"Well, that's dangerous," Diane said to Molly's back. Molly had braided her hair starting from the crown of her head in a sort of basket-weave pattern, and a single brown pigtail, secured by a rubber band, dangled. "They could chew through wires and start a fire. Does the landlord know?"

Once more Molly curled inward and the pigtail flopped on the linoleum. "He said he was going to call an exterminator," she muttered. "I told him not to."

"Whyever not?"

She unwound herself and said, stiffening her spine, "I don't want animals dying of poison all around me."

"You'd rather the whole house went up in flames, I suppose."

Molly hopped up from the rug and walked across the room to the refrigerator. "Don't worry, I've got a smoke alarm. Any day I'm going to get batteries for it."

"Any *day?*"

"Tomorrow, Mom. I promise." As she gazed into the refrigerator Molly yanked her leotards down over her behind. She's so solid, Diane thought. Where did that earthly substance come from? Feet slapping on the floor, Molly carried a bottle of supermarket wine to the table. Lint from the rag rug adhered to her leotards. "This was left over from a party," Molly said. "Want some?"

"I'm on a diet."

"What for?"

"I'm not over the hill quite yet."

"Who said you were?"

"Maybe a drop. I have to go soon, though. The Camry's in the shop. Blocked fuel line or something, so I have to pick Todd up at work."

"Oh, right. Todd." *Todd the bod. Todd the clod.* Molly poured wine into two juice glasses. She handed one to her mother, who minced over to the couch on tippy-toes and sat on one end of it. Her polo coat gaped open. Molly noticed a coil of fat pushed up by the waistband of her mother's trousers, visible under her green silk shirt. Suddenly Molly remembered a vase she'd made in summer camp one rainy day, coiling a snake of clay round and round and then pressing the clay smooth with her fingers. "Hey, whatever happened to that vase I made at camp?" she asked.

"Vase?" With her fingernail Diane lifted a speck off the surface of her wine. "What was it like?"

"Dark green. Trumpet-shaped."

"I think it's coming back to me."

"You never used that vase." Molly sat in a kitchen chair and set her glass on the table. "You never put flowers in it."

"Oh Molly, I didn't want to tell you, but it leaked. There was a tiny hole at the base. The first time I used it, water spilled all over."

"So what did you do, pitch it in the trash?"

"Of course not." Diane tasted her wine and tried not to wince. "Maybe it broke one of the times we moved, I'm not sure. Have you been holding a grudge all this time?"

"I haven't thought of the vase in years." Though that was true, Molly felt anger like crystals of Drano start to burn in her chest.

Diane combed her fingers through her hair, leaving scrubby bleached furrows. "I get tired of your grudges, Molly. Really tired."

Elaine Ford

"That was the summer," Molly said, "things began to go down the tubes."

"What summer?"

"That's why you dumped me at camp."

"Oh no, Molly, you can't lay that on me. You *wanted* to go to that camp. Horse camp. You were crazy about horses, you had horses on the brain."

"I have this very clear picture in my head. We were sitting out on the deck, you and me, eating breakfast. Cream cheese on bagels. Caterpillars kept falling out of the chestnut tree onto the cream cheese. You opened the back of the *Times* magazine section and said, 'Pick a camp. Any camp.' Dad was away somewhere."

"That's not at all way it was. Your little friend—the one who lived in the cul-de-sac, Heather?—she was the one who got you all fired up about going to camp."

"I never," Molly said, picking up a fork from the table and beginning to clean grime out from underneath her toenails, "had a friend named Heather. I never had a friend at all in that cul-de-sac."

"Molly, sometimes I think you inhabit some world other than the real one."

"I live in the real one, all right." Molly stared at her toes. Not very well designed, the way the nail of one tended to poke into the skin of the one next to it.

"Well," Diane said, "it's true your father had a girlfriend that summer." She drank some of her wine. It no longer tasted quite so much like nail polish remover, now that it had had a chance to breathe some. "Stupid girl who worked in a flower shop. Later on she married an undertaker, I heard. Of course, she wasn't the issue."

"Why not?"

"Maybe it would be closer to the truth to say I refused to let her be the issue."

"I don't understand." Molly looked at her mother. Bleached hair, *champagne* the shade on the package label, frizzy from an indifferent perm. Fake gold costume jewelry. Rayon slacks. How could Molly have come from this person's womb?

"You know how people who fight in wars want there to be a reason for the war? A moral reason, I mean, not just some dumb dispute over a piece of land? So if they die, there's some point to it?"

"What are you talking about?"

"I swore if my marriage was going to bite the dust it was going to be over something important."

"Yeah? Like what?"

"Like being in charge of my own life for a change."

"But it was my life, too," Molly said quietly.

"I never forgot that, Molly. Not for a single second."

Molly wiped the fork on her leotards. "But then *Todd* came along. Out there in the trenches morals get kind of lost, it seems."

"You don't know," Diane said. "You have no right to judge."

"Sure. Judge not, that ye be not judged. That's what they taught us in Sunday School."

Diane emptied her glass. She walked to the counter and placed it next to the bag of groceries. Out of the corner of her eye she saw, or thought she saw, something skitter into the crevice between counter and wall. She turned and said, "Oh, why don't you just come home? Give it a try?"

"No. I don't think so."

Soon Molly heard her mother's footsteps on the stairs. The squirrels were quiet, maybe curled in their nests. She stood on the cool linoleum and shut her eyes. In her mind she saw the peak of the attic, each nail holding sheetrock securely against a beam. She concentrated on the crack where the panels of sheetrock came together. After a while she no longer felt grit under her feet.

RITA LAFFERTY'S LUCKY SUMMER

The summer I was sixteen I had my first real job, selling pastries in Jojo's Bakery on Broadway, near Sullivan Square. Over the machine that dispensed tickets was a hand-lettered sign: *Take a Number.* Like my Aunt Grace saying, "Take a card, take a card," when she was going to do a trick or tell my fortune. Maybe the ticket machine was a lucky number machine, I liked to think. When I called out "seventeen" or "fifty-three" to the customers waiting their turn to be served, I half expected one of them to wave her ticket and shout "Bingo!" Nobody ever did, though. They'd be trying to shush their yammering kid or figuring out whether one pineapple cake could be sliced thin enough to feed eleven people.

It was hard work. On your feet all day and no goofing off; whenever the stream of customers thinned out Jojo would always find something for you to do in back, washing cookie trays or making up boxes. What I really wanted to do was work the pastry tube, but no chance of that.

Rita Lafferty, who worked at Jojo's with me, fell in love that summer. Rita was thirty, though she didn't look it. Her teeth were as bucked as though she'd spent her childhood opening tonic bottles with them. She lived with her mother over on Fosket Street. Mrs. Lafferty was forever calling up the bakery, trying to talk Rita into leaving early so she could run some errand for her. She'd even have made up the excuse that Rita was supposed to tell Jojo. Poor Rita didn't know whether to be more afraid of her mother or of getting fired.

The best thing about Rita was her hair. It was reddish brown and so heavy and dense that even the awful hair nets we had to wear couldn't squash it. Once she made me examine the roots to prove to me that the color came from God. Not that I'd suspected otherwise.

Rita's boyfriend was a motorman on the Orange Line; he spent his working hours riding from Oak Grove to Forest Hills and back. They'd met in the Star Market, when he dropped a can of cream-style corn on her toe. He was a bachelor who lived alone in Magoun Square and cooked for himself. His name was Frank Hodges.

Rita limped around for a few days, smiling goofily whenever anyone asked how she'd hurt her foot. And then, the day Frank's gift arrived at the bakery, she began to confide in me.

He'd sent it to apologize—possibly to head off a suit, though I didn't suggest that to Rita: a large ceramic donkey with a clump of geraniums in each raffia saddle basket. "Isn't it cunning?" she said. And how had Frank guessed that geraniums were practically her favorite flower?

"Maybe he thought they'd match your hair?" I offered. The donkey had a somewhat toothy expression, but I didn't mention that to Rita, either.

"My hair's not *that* kind of red. Still, to men red is red."

"That's what I mean," I agreed, from my own extensive knowledge of men.

"He asked me out," Rita went on, "when I called to thank him."

"How did you know his number?"

She looked only a little sheepish. "I looked it up in the phone book. Well, I *had* to thank him, didn't I?"

They went to the movies that weekend, and the next weekend, on a Sunday afternoon, to Fenway Park to jeer at Don Zimmer. Finally, Frank came around to the bakery. He turned out to be a better-looking man than you'd imagine Rita could catch, even with her great hair. Not tall, but plenty of muscles and so tan you'd have thought he spent every day stretched out on Revere Beach instead of inside a subway car. Maybe not quite as old as Rita, but it was hard to tell for sure.

"He seems nice," I told her later, as we were bringing out trays of cream puffs. Rita only smiled. When she kept her mouth shut, she was surprisingly pretty. Especially after Frank came into her life. I began to notice things. She had nice breasts—we'd strip out of our nylon uniforms at the end of the day, the two of us crowded into the tiny john in back—and she had a kind of sexy smell about her, too. Not that she was *sleeping* with Frank, I was sure, but her excitement was there in her delicate sweat and in the new way she moved her body. She even talked back to Mrs. Lafferty once or twice when the old witch called, demanding to know how soon she'd be home.

Now I began to wonder why no man had noticed Rita before, why she had seemed so obviously virginal and fated to remain that way. Of course, there was the buck teeth. And she did tend to giggle, particularly in a crisis, and she fell all over herself agreeing with you, no matter what outrageous thing you'd said. Still, look outside the plate glass window onto Broadway: women walking by who are unmistakably married—someone once made love to them and planted babies in them—and how all that happened is a mystery. Arms puckered with fat now, gold teeth and false gold hair, voices like fishwives.

Frank started picking Rita up after work. He drove a yellow Corvette, only slightly dented. The car worried me a little, because I calculated what it must cost to keep up the payments and wondered whether there'd be enough left over to support a wife, let alone babies and a mother-in-law. They'd gone to Virgie's, she'd tell me the next morning, or to Davis Square for a pizza.

"How come Frank is always available to pick you up?" I asked her. "Whether you work till 4:30 or 7:30 he always manages to be here."

"He arranges his schedule around mine," she said, gazing at the birthday cake display. For some reason the glass on that particular case makes a good mirror.

"How can he do that?"

She smiled, tucking a few wisps of hair into her hair net and letting the elastic snap. "He has a lot of seniority. He gets first crack at the work sheet."

Well, I believed it if she did.

And then all at once it struck me that she *was* sleeping with him, after all. There were no more reports of what movie they'd seen, or what they'd had to eat at Virgie's. If I asked her, she'd say, "Oh, I forget." Rita was a terrible liar, no inventiveness, no acting ability. I imagined them in Frank's steamy apartment, making love to the rattle of traffic in Magoun Square, and I feared for her soul.

Then Rita showed me the ring, her engagement ring. Frank had bought it downtown on Washington Street and made a very good bargain, she told me. Diamond solitaire, one-quarter carat, platinum setting. They planned on an October wedding, she said shyly.

I was happy for her. At least, I hoped, Mrs. Lafferty would have to start hewing and drawing for herself once in awhile.

The Saturday after Rita confided to me her wedding plans Frank failed to pick her up. Ordinarily I would have left her waiting in front of Jojo's without giving it a thought, but that day she had the curse. Rita was afflicted with theatrical, extravagant menstrual flows, during which her body seemed bent on flushing out her entire blood supply. Since she looked a little shaky I lingered with her, watching for that sleek yellow vehicle to come zipping along from Magoun Square.

No Corvette. Rita twisted the engagement ring around her finger. A fidgety rain began to fall. It got to be 7:40, then ten of.

"What do you think I should do?" she asked me finally.

At that moment I spotted the Number 89 bus moving slowly in the traffic, heading west out of Sullivan Square. I grabbed her arm and pulled her across Broadway to the bus stop in front of the firehouse. "We'll go over to Frank's place and see what's up. Maybe he's sick," I said.

"Shouldn't we call first?"

I gave her an exasperated look. If she'd been in his bed every night for a month, did she have to call first before visiting him? "There won't be another bus for forty minutes," I said.

His apartment was a third floor walk-up over a sub shop. We rang his bell, and when there was no answer I pushed the street door open and we went upstairs, past bicycles and strollers on the landings.

"Which door is Frank's?" I asked her.

She pointed it out, knowing she was compromised, but seeing no alternative. I guess she was grateful to have me take charge.

I knocked. We could hear staticky music from inside, but nobody came to the door. "Well, now what?"

Without saying anything, she dug around in her handbag and came up with the key.

For a bachelor Frank was neat as a pin, I'll have to give him that. Everything was in place: plastic tablecloth on the table, sofa cover free of wrinkles.

As in a trance, Rita walked into the bedroom, and I came behind her. Frank was lying on the bed, out cold. The radio signal had shifted since he'd tuned it in. An empty bottle sat on the bed next to the radio.

"He drinks," she breathed.

"Let's go, Rita."

"No, you go. I'll stay with him."

"Come on, Rita." I pulled at her arm.

"No, it's all right," she said. I saw the buck teeth when she spoke. She didn't giggle, even though it was a crisis, and she settled down to watch over him.

I think they got married, though I'm not sure. After I quit working at Jojo's to go back to school I never heard from Rita, and I never ran into her on the street. Probably she and Frank moved to Stoneham or Billerica, the better to escape Mrs. Lafferty.

COUSINS

Coming home, Edie feels as if she has drunk from the White Rabbit's bottle and grown so huge that her spine is jammed against the doorknob, an arm is hanging out the window, a knee is up the chimney. Each time she visits, the ceilings seem lower and the rooms more cramped. Edie's mother, always a small woman, has shrunk even smaller.

Edie squeezes between chair and dining table at her old place. "They make you walk more miles in the terminal," she says, "than you fly to get there. It's great to sit down."

Her mother has prepared iced tea, although it's early November and the house is frugally heated. Stirring her tea, she asks, "How long are you going to stay this time?"

By letter and over the phone, Edie has already explained that she'll be here a week. The office will plunge into disarray without her: contracts and deeds mysteriously vanishing, important clients left dangling on hold or cut off altogether, attorneys finding themselves in court without some crucial evidentiary document in their possession. Anyway, a week is about as much as Edie can stand. Patiently she says, "Until next Monday. What would you like to do while I'm here? I thought we might drive over to the new mall one day."

"Mall? I don't need to buy anything at a mall."

"Just for fun, to look around. We could have lunch somewhere nice afterward."

"I do not, Edith, need to be taken on excursions like a child."

In her old age, Edie's mother has largely dispensed with politeness, in what Edie thinks of as a conservation-of-energy move. Or possibly, because of her mother's poor eyesight, the dismayed expressions of others no longer register. She's free to do as she pleases.

"You'd better go see your cousin Arlene," her mother says briskly.

"I doubt that Arlene wants to see me, any more than I want to see her."

"You might not get another chance."

"What—are they retiring to the Bahamas?" Joke. Nobody's more wedded to territory and habit than Arlene and Paul. They've lived their entire lives in this town, closing in on six decades.

"She's got cancer."

Edie is too stunned to reply. Outside on the lawn grackles are pecking in the stiff brown grass. Bushes along the property line need pruning. The garage roof is missing some shingles.

"Lung cancer."

"Where is she? Home? The hospital?"

"Not surprising, the way she's always smoked."

"I'll go see her tomorrow," Edie promises.

June, 1952. They told their mothers they had to work on a history project, a group report on Mesopotamia, at the home of one of their classmates. In order to be believed, according to Arlene, it was essential to act like a victim—no, *be* a victim. Edie did her best. "We have to write a two-thousand-word essay," she complained to her mother, "and make a relief map out of papier-mâché."

From the ironing board her mother gave her a glance that might have been interpreted as skeptical and said, "I'm glad Arlene is so serious about this assignment." She flipped the shirt over and attacked the collar. "For once."

Early that Saturday morning the cousins joined up at the bus terminal, a scarred bench inside a shelter made of concrete, and waited to catch the #36. On weekdays the bus came every half hour, picking up commuters to take them into Manhattan in the mornings and then, in the evenings, dumping them back in town. On weekends the bus ran only once an hour. "Pray to God we didn't miss it," Arlene said. She groped in her purse for cigarettes.

But right on time the dirty red bus appeared, like the devil when you call his name, and they were aboard. Arlene was wearing her church pumps, freshly whitened, her legs bare. Narrow, knee-length navy skirt with a kick pleat, sleeveless blouse. Her dark hair she'd skinned back into a pony tail. She looked much older than thirteen, Edie thought, especially once she'd applied her lipstick and Cover Girl, almost old enough to be served beer across the state line. Arlene had what *Seventeen* magazine called "poise," and Edie felt proud to be in her company.

The summer before, in Arlene's kitchen, while her mother was out grocery shopping, the cousins had made shallow cuts in their thighs, pinched the cuts until the blood ran, and with their thumbs mixed their blood together. "Friends to the death," Arlene had sworn. Knowing that Arlene's blood ran in her veins along with her own made Edie feel bolder, cleverer, more alive.

"We're gonna be famous," Arlene said, double-checking to make sure the complimentary tickets were safely stowed in her purse. The first event on the day's agenda was to be a live television broadcast, a two-hour variety show. The show's host, Dick Nickles, would intermittently bring people from the studio audience up on stage to chat with him and the guest celebrities at a breakfast table. As they rode along, Arlene rehearsed the witty rejoinders she'd pre-pared for when she was on television. *So how do you like junior high? If I was high, I'd like it a whole lot better. What's your favorite hobby? Well, Dick, I'll give you a hint. It ain't bowling, and it ain't Ping-Pong.*

Suddenly it struck Edie that what had for months been a fantasy of romantic adventure, endlessly embellished in their shared imagina-tions, was becoming reality at exactly the same speed that the bus was barreling toward the George Washington Bridge. Scary reality. "How will we explain it?" Edie asked. "Being on television in New York when we're supposed to be at Brenda Kling's house making a relief map out of papier-mâché?"

"Are you nuts? Everybody in town will be talking about us. Who'll care about Mesopotamia then?"

My mother, Edie thought. "Maybe this isn't such a good idea."

"For Crissake, don't be such a stick-in-the-mud." The bus spewed exhaust fumes. Suburban New Jersey lurched past the window.

After the breakfast show, the plan was, they'd have banana splits for lunch. Then back on the subway and on to Radio City Music Hall for the matinee: Elizabeth Taylor in *Ivanhoe*. Arlene wasn't in the least worried about negotiating the subways. You get lost, you ask somebody for directions, simple as that.

As it happened, Dick Nickles did not invite them to come up and drink coffee at his breakfast table. They could hardly even see the table from where their seats were, off to one side, bulky equipment in the way. All they could observe without interference was the flashing red light signaling them when to applaud. No famous movie stars were on the show today, just an ancient guy they never heard of. He cracked some feeble jokes and did a tap-dance. Arlene whispered that she hoped he'd have a stroke and fall dead on the stage. It would be a lot more exciting than his act.

The studio guests who were called on stage and interviewed on television were a couple from Iowa who had been married sixty years and an insurance salesman from Minnesota who, after enthusiastic prompting from Dick Nickles, demonstrated bird calls. Loons. Whippoorwills. At home during the two hours the show ran you'd be washing dishes, talking on the telephone, doing your homework, running the vacuum cleaner—half the time not even in the same room as the television set. Here, in the studio audience, you were trapped. When a woman did a floor wax commercial and the camera wasn't on him, Dick Nickles looked old and depressed, Edie noticed.

The banana splits for lunch weren't that great, though neither Edie nor Arlene said so. They had to wait a long time at a busy lunch counter, and when finally they were served, the bananas under the balls of ice cream and the marshmallow sauce were overripe—rotten, actually. Edie began to feel queasy a third of the way through her banana split, but decided she'd better eat the whole thing because it had been so expensive and so Arlene wouldn't be disgusted with her. *What's the point of doing anything with you? You're hopeless.*

They boarded a subway train that hurtled them out to some mysterious borough, where the tracks elevated into daylight, exposing grim and filthy buildings with people staring blankly out of windows. By the time they figured out what was wrong and got back to where they'd started, they were so late for the show at Radio City Music Hall that they missed the Rockettes and the first half hour of *Ivanhoe*. Edie never did quite get the hang of the plot.

"Why did you follow me onto that train like a sheep?" Arlene demanded afterward. Crowds of suburban ladies and tourists shoved past them in the lobby.

Wounded, Edie said, "I told you it was the wrong one. You wouldn't listen."

On the sidewalk Arlene yanked cigarettes out of her purse and lit one, without offering the pack to Edie. Edie saw that Arlene was limping, the backs of her sockless heels raw with blisters. Edie herself had a terrible headache.

Sullenly they found their way to the uptown terminal, and then home on the #36. "You going to tell?" Arlene asked.

"No." She could keep a secret as well as Arlene. Better.

However, a whole week passed before Arlene could coax Edie into going over to her house to read movie magazines and talk about boys and sit on the edge of the tub, smoking, with the bathroom window open.

"I know what you're thinking," Arlene says. "You're wondering how I can still do it." Her arm tucked in tight to her chest, she studies the lit cigarette gripped between thumb and forefinger. "God knows I don't want to. Long and short of it is, I don't have your guts."

Edie looks at the carpet, a floral oriental that once covered the parlor floor of their grandmother Mallory's house on Grant Street. In this house, a tract colonial built in the early sixties, the rug looks garishly busy. "I don't know about guts," Edie replies.

"You quit."

"I never liked smoking much. I did it because you did."

"That was a dumb reason," Arlene says. She laughs and takes a final drag off her cigarette, then hammers it into the ashtray.

On the walk over to Circle Drive, Edie wondered whether Arlene had lost her hair from chemotherapy. Would she wear some kind of a hat or scarf? Or find it amusing to present herself to Edie bald as a darning egg? Arlene does have hair, however—almost shoulder length, uncombed, gray strands mixed in with the brown. She's lost an alarming amount of weight. The whites of her eyes look tobacco-stained.

"I only just heard," Edie says. "Yesterday."

In the ashtray, a choked wisp of smoke struggles upward from the smashed cigarette. Arlene says, "It ain't good." Their eyes meet. "The tumor's spread to the lung lining, so they can't operate. Or do radiation, either. The chemo made me throw up so much they had to stop. I have to get my strength back before they can try another kind."

"I wish I knew how to help you."

Arlene lifts a bony shoulder. "You could donate a lung—or better yet, two. Sign right here on the dotted line."

"Arlene . . ."

"The whole family thinks I'm a goner, and not only that, I have it coming to me. For smoking like a chimney plus the multitude of other sins I have or may have committed." She coughs harshly and spits something into a tissue, which she folds up as though it contains some treasure worth preserving. Then she grins at Edie. "But I fully intend to confound you all."

"I believe you."

To Edie's relief they begin to talk about Arlene's kids, long since grown up and moved away. Debbie's a travel agent, Russell a high-school social studies teacher and swimming coach. "Neither of them married," Arlene says, "or look much like they're going to. No doubt that reflects on me." Without waiting for a response she goes on, "Neither of them interested in hustling Dodges, either. Not that I blame them. I don't know what's going to happen to the business when Paul retires."

"He's not ready to retire yet, is he?" Edie asks.

"Lately he's been talking about it. Hard to tell how serious he is."

Neither speaks for a few moments. Then Arlene says, "I bet you wonder what he's like now."

"Who, Paul?"

Arlene has lit another cigarette. She seems to exhale from a pit so deep in her chest that Edie pictures violently detached tumor cells spewing out of her nose and mouth, settling on the furniture and on Edie's skin like thick, chalky, malignant dust.

"Of course, Paul. Who else?" Arlene asks.

"It's not as though I haven't seen him in these years, you know. Millie's funeral and . . ."

Arlene smiles, fingering the cigarette. "No, I mean *really* like, on the inside. You're curious, aren't you."

"I haven't thought about it."

"If you say so."

The Paul Edie knew was eighteen years old. Read dictionaries for the fun of it, spoke convincingly of doing something with his life. Forty years ago Edie gave him up, turned her back on him. Arlene's right, though. Paul still has some hold on her.

"I want to show you something." Arlene lifts herself from her chair, and Edie sees how weak she is, realizes for the first time that she's in pain. Edie imagines a sensation like huge metal staples in the bad lung, cutting into tissue, cutting off breath.

She follows her cousin to a door in the hallway and they descend a flight of steps. Arlene moves gingerly, holding tight onto the railing. Even before they reach bottom, Edie can see that in the basement is— improbably but undeniably—an airplane. Not a model, the real thing. "Good God," she says. The plane, something like a Piper Cub, Edie supposes, is in the process of construction. On a work table chunks of the innards lie partially assembled; gauges and other mechanical components sprout tangles of wires. Positioned between the basement's support beams, the plane's shell seems complete, or nearly so: wings, fuselage, bubble cockpit, tail. The wing span must be twenty-five or thirty feet, stretching almost the entire length of the basement.

"He's making it from a kit," Arlene says. "Been working on the goddamn thing forever. This is all he does, when he's not at work."

"I can't believe my mother hasn't mentioned it."

Arlene laughs. "Nobody has a clue, including Russ and Debbie. When they're here for Thanksgiving or some other holiday he keeps the cellar door locked—not that they'd have any reason to come down here. They're not apt to go hunting for a tool to make some little repair around the house."

The only way out of the basement, except for the steps they've come down, is a bulkhead through which one might wedge at most a washing machine or maybe an old sofa bed, with considerable angling and grunting. How in the world is Paul going to get the plane out of here when it's finished?

"He'd kill me if he knew I'm showing it to you," Arlene says.

"Then why are you?"

"You really don't get it?"

"No. I don't."

"Then I guess I'll have to spell it out for you. Paul wasn't any great bargain, Edie. You didn't miss a thing."

April, 1957. They'd gone steady for two years, since they were sophomores. Edie wore his class ring on a chain around her neck.

Usually, on a Saturday night, Paul would drive her straight home after the double feature at the Grand. He'd have been up practically before dawn that morning and run at least five miles before working all day at his father's dealership. Tonight, though, instead of heading across the railroad tracks and out County Road, he pulled into the Mister Softee parking lot. "Would you like a cone?" he asked. "Or a shake?" He turned off the key in the ignition.

"No thanks," Edie said, puzzled.

"I don't know, I feel like I want something." He got out of the car, kicking the door shut behind him, and strode over to the counter window. In Mister Softee's fluorescent lighting his sensitive, handsome face looked harsh, his eyes unreadable hollows. For a while he stared at the posted menu, but returned without buying anything. "Nothing sounded good to me," he said.

She thought he'd start the car then, but he just sat behind the wheel as if in a daze. The truth was, for the last couple of months Paul had regularly seemed off in some other world. Restless, irritable. She'd assumed it was the state and regional track competitions coming up. She knew he wanted to win some medals before graduation, his last crack at glory. Or possibly his parents were putting some kind of pressure on him. Or—could it be?—maybe he wanted to break up with her, but was afraid to say so.

"Do you have something to tell me?" she asked.

"I don't know, Edie. I don't know if I can."

They sat in the rusty Dodge his dad had acquired on a trade-in, while customers drove in and ordered food and drove off again. She heard the clock on the Union Dime strike the half hour. Her mother would be wondering why she wasn't home yet, might even be calling Paul's parents. Car by car the Mister Softee parking lot emptied, until they were the only ones there.

"One night," he said finally, "around nine-thirty, I was just finishing up my physics homework. The telephone rang. This was back in February, I think. Icy patches on the roads, still."

He paused for such a long time that Edie had to ask, "Well, who was on the phone?"

"Your cousin. Arlene. She needed to talk to me, she said."

"To you?" Edie asked in amazement. Although classmates, those two might as well have been at opposite poles on the planet: shy, bookish Paul and life-of-the-party Arlene. After Paul and Edie began dating, she'd been drawn into his group of friends—other long-distance runners, guys with hobbies like beekeeping and model building, writers for the school paper. The Girl Scouts, Arlene called them contemptuously. Edie pretended not to care what Arlene thought, but of course she did. "Why you?"

"She explained that this . . . thing . . . wasn't something Edie would understand."

"Oh, I see."

"She asked me to go over to her house," Paul said.

"Just like that? Nine-thirty at night?"

He picked at a cuticle. "She ran out of the house to meet me. We couldn't talk there," Paul continued, "because of her parents. So we went for a drive."

"Where?"

He acted as if he didn't understand the question. "Where?"

"Where did you drive to?"

"The reservoir. What difference does it make?"

"I just wondered."

"After we got there Arlene took a couple of beers out of her bag, the big plastic beach bag she carries around."

"I know the one."

"I didn't want to drink, but she pried the caps off and shoved one of the beers at me. She drank about half of hers, guzzling it down. Then she started to talk about how awful she felt, and how much she hated herself."

"Was she drinking before you picked her up?"

"I don't think so. I didn't smell it on her breath. Anyway, something had her worked up, that's for sure. People didn't really like her, she said, they only pretended to. I told her that wasn't true, she was just imagining it, and then she said she wished she had the nerve to kill herself."

Melodrama, Arlene's specialty, Edie thought uneasily.

"She sounded serious, but I wasn't sure whether to believe her or not. I tried to laugh her out of it: What, and miss the prom, Arlene?

"All that accomplished was to make her furious. She smashed her bottle against the dashboard and was going to jam it into her wrist, but her coat sleeve was in the way. We wrestled over the bottle and I managed to get it away from her—I don't know why we weren't cut to ribbons. Both of us drenched in beer, broken glass everywhere. Arlene was crying and laughing and swearing, grabbing onto me and struggling to get away from me, all at the same time." He stared out the window, at the Mister Softee stand. "That's when I went crazy, I guess."

Crazy? What did he mean? And then she knew. "You don't have to say anything more."

"I was so wound up," Paul said. "I couldn't stop."

She realized that deep down she'd been expecting something like this to happen, right from the beginning. Since they were toddlers in the same playpen, Arlene had always managed to get her hands on Edie's toys. The wonder was that Arlene hadn't tampered with Edie and Paul before now. "Is she pregnant?" Edie's voice sounded calm to her own ears, mildly curious.

"No," he said. "We were lucky."

We were lucky. As if they'd become a kind of couple, bound together in their craziness and recklessness and undeserved luck. Edie had never even let Paul unbutton her blouse, although she'd wanted him to.

She thought about slivers of glass driven into the Dodge's grubby upholstery by the force of Arlene's fake anguish. Eventually the bits of glass would work their way to the surface, like splinters in skin.

"I'm sorry, Edie."

"It doesn't matter," she said. "We'll forget about it."

But it did matter, and she couldn't forget about it. Not so much that Paul had done this inexplicable thing, but that the one in his car out at the reservoir had been Arlene. Her own blood relation. The person in Edie's life she'd most envied, admired, and been tormented by.

What kind of pill could you take for pain like this? Not aspirin, not Anacin. It was as if she'd been whacked in the chest with a shovel and couldn't breathe. After a week she gave Paul's ring back to him. He said little in response, except that she had to be the one to decide. Without him she felt miserably alone and desperate for his comfort. At the same time she wanted him to be hurt as much as he'd hurt her.

Her feelings seemed to Edie like rubbery brown toadstools,

springing up relentlessly in swampy ground. She almost wished Arlene hadn't been faking—that she'd meant her threat, and one day she'd be gone. Then Edie wouldn't have to hear her raucous laughter in the corridors and see her hanging around the lockers with her brainless friends.

But even if Arlene were to disappear off the face of the Earth tomorrow, everything would still be spoiled. Edie thought she'd never trust anyone again.

The summer after graduation she worked in the town office, filing documents and running the mimeograph machine. Sometimes when she walked by the Dodge dealership, she'd see Paul outside in the lot, hosing down a used car or screwing plates onto a shiny new vehicle. Though they gave no sign of noticing one another, she had the sense that his eyes followed her as she crossed the street and went into the A&P. Arlene, Edie heard, was going out with a guy from the next town who played drums in a rock 'n' roll band.

In the fall, rather than entering the community college along with Paul and Arlene, Edie took the bus into Manhattan and attended a secretarial course. She learned typing, shorthand, and bookkeeping, and came out first in her class. The school put a short item about her success in the local newspaper. No one called up to congratulate her, no one she cared about.

Right out of school Edie was hired by a small Wall Street law firm and, relieved she could afford to stop riding the bus and living at home, rented a tiny studio apartment on the Upper West Side. That November, while clearing leaves from a gutter, Paul's father suffered a heart attack and fell to his death from an extension ladder. Edie wrote Paul a brief condolence note on linen-textured paper she bought for the purpose, but decided against attending the funeral. Within a few weeks she heard from her mother that he'd dropped out of college to take over his father's business. Arlene turned up, late, at the family Christmas Eve party and broadcast the news that she'd also dropped out of school, at the end of the fall semester, and was going to work part-time at the Dodge dealership—doing what, Edie couldn't imagine. Arlene didn't know how to type with more than two fingers, and the idea of her balancing books was laughable. She chattered about her new boyfriend, Rog, who did not make an appearance at the party.

After a year in the law firm, Edie married Si Weinfeld, an attorney who might modestly mention, after a drink or two, that he'd clerked for Felix Frankfurter. The following year Si received an excellent job offer in Chicago, and they moved there.

Her husband was politically liberal, of conservative disposition, narrow-hipped, sparse-haired, more than twice her age. He earned many times what Paul could possibly be making selling Dodges in a small New Jersey town.

Edie did not return East for Paul and Arlene's wedding. "Si just can't find the time," Edie explained to the family. "His schedule's incredibly hectic." As if to authenticate her excuse, within months Si was appointed to a federal district court judgeship.

For one reason and another, Edie's marriage didn't survive. After the divorce she stayed in Chicago. "I don't understand. You hate the weather out there," her mother kept saying over the phone. Yes. Foul winters, summers like the interior of an oven. But by now Edie had a circle of supportive friends there, a challenging job that paid enough for her to live comfortably, season tickets to the symphony—a life. And she couldn't bear the thought of going home.

From the closet in her bedroom Edie has to drag out a portable sewing machine and several cartons of china inherited from Grandma Mallory to get to it: a cardboard box she packed away the summer after she graduated from high school. She has not opened it since.

She wipes dust from the box, which is somewhat squashed from having had other boxes piled on top of it, and uses her thumbnail to slit the peeling tape. Inside are her yearbook; the collection of Shakespeare's sonnets presented to her for having won the prize in English composition—she never read them, knowing by then she wasn't going on to college; bundles of letters and postcards from various relatives, collected throughout her childhood—why in the world had she saved them? *Dear Edie, here we are writing to you from Sea Girt, everybody sunburned, hope you are having fun with your new goldfish, how is vacation Bible school?* A scrapbook of autographed photos begged by mail from movie stars, which she and Arlene assembled in seventh grade. Cute Debbie Reynolds, before Eddie Fisher abandoned her for Elizabeth Taylor. Perky Carleton Carpenter, Debbie's dancing partner—who remembers him now? The tassel from Edie's graduation cap, the silk tangled and yellowed. No crumbling corsage from the senior prom, because she wouldn't go with Paul. Arlene went with Tom Machan, who afterward got a girl pregnant and had to marry her. Scandal at the time. Nobody would think twice about it now.

What she's looking for is at the bottom of the box. Edie had buried it there deliberately, as an alternative to burning it: a thin pile of deckle-edged snapshots, tied together with a piece of string. Saturday afternoon, early fall of their sophomore year. 1954, it would have been. They'd ridden their bikes out to the reservoir, seven or eight miles from town. There is Paul, his back against a tree, he and the tree leaning at an angle because she hadn't held the camera quite straight. Lopsided grin, attractive intelligent face. And there is Edie: that cable-knit sweater that she loved, long straight hair flying in the wind, hands clasped. Eyes intent on the tall boy holding her Brownie camera. *Cheese,* he said, but she didn't smile, can't remember why now.

They'd walked along the edge of the reservoir and taken more snapshots. Of the landscape, which looks dull and washed out in black and white, but wasn't. Of each other.

He kissed her for the first time, cradling her face between his large gentle hands. Of course there is no photographic record of that moment.

Without knocking, her mother enters Edie's room. The old woman's cropped hair is awry; her too-large mannish cardigan bears stains she can't see because of her failing eyesight or else doesn't care are there. "Good," she says cheerfully. "About time you cleared your junk out of that closet. I can use the storage space."

Edie is in the drugstore to buy hand lotion. She sees Paul standing at the magazine rack, thumbing through a copy of *Popular Science*. He doesn't look much changed from the last time, at Millie's funeral, three or four years ago. Still has most of his hair, though it's entirely gray, and is still a careful dresser, for this dumpy suburban town. Sports jacket, neatly pressed khakis. She has an idea Arlene wouldn't have done the pressing, even before the cancer. Possibly Paul's tall frame is a little stooped now.

She'll just sidle up to the checkout, Edie thinks, and leave quietly with the Jergens. What does she have to say to him? But he looks up from the magazine and recognition animates his expressive face. Perhaps he, too, wishes he could flee unnoticed. But now it isn't possible.

Paul moves toward her, still holding the magazine. "I didn't know you were in town," he says. "It's good to see you, Edie." He clears his throat. "I guess your mother must have . . ."

Edie nods. She wonders whether she should tell him that she visited Arlene yesterday. If Arlene didn't bring it up, she must have her reasons. On the other hand, if Edie plays dumb, and Arlene mentions it casually at dinner tonight, Edie will look devious or foolish or both.

Absently he's rolling and unrolling the *Popular Science*. How can he return it to the rack in that condition? "Where are you headed?" he asks.

"Home."

"On foot?"

"I didn't trust my mother's old Chrysler."

"I could give her a good deal on a Neon. Or maybe an Intrepid."

"I don't think we want to encourage her to drive."

He smiles his lopsided smile. "Mind if I walk part way with you?"

She pays for the lotion and he, surprised to find himself holding the magazine, pays for the manhandled *Popular Science*. Then they are on the sidewalk. The November air is chilly, with a hint of snow. Too soon, Edie thinks. Damp leaves stick to their feet as they pass the Union Dime, which now has a glass-walled ATM booth attached to the old sandstone, and a hole-in-the-wall Thai restaurant, where the United Cigar Store used to be.

"That place any good?" she asks.

"Haven't tried it. Arlene won't eat Oriental food."

"I saw her yesterday," Edie confesses.

"You were over at the house?"

"For an hour. In the afternoon."

"She didn't tell me."

They round the corner. The Mister Softee stand has long since been torn down, its asphalt parking lot dug up and replaced by a little park, which has in turn fallen on hard times, no longer funded by town officials. Frozen weeds crowd shriveled phlox and chrysanthemums. Rusty chains, missing their seats, dangle from a swing set.

They have crossed the railroad tracks and are heading out of downtown, north on County Road, before she speaks again. "It must be very difficult for you," she says.

"Difficult isn't the word."

She glances up at his face. Strange the way the years coarsen the features, flatten the nose and thicken the flesh below the mouth as if with layers of weather insulation. If only the protection worked.

"The cancer would be bad enough." He tightens his hands on the rolled magazine. "But what's worse, almost, is the way she shuts me out."

Edie wishes she'd driven the decrepit Chrysler, for all its eccentricities, instead of insisting to her mother that a walk would do her good. She's not eager to have to contemplate the internal workings of Paul's marriage.

"She makes everything so hard," he says. "I feel like I've stumbled into a play that only Arlene knows the lines to. Not that that's anything new."

Overhead, a nearly invisible jet is tracing a gleaming pencil line in the sky at above the speed of sound. As they watch, the stream broadens and thins out, stippling in air currents, finally teased like frail wisps of cotton batting into the atmosphere.

As if ashamed of how much he's revealed to Edie, he says, "She can't help it that she's sick. She can't help the way she is."

"None of us can," Edie agrees.

On a front stoop is a jack-o'-lantern that the frost must have gotten to, puckering its face and caving in its teeth. For no reason Edie says, "I used to smoke with her. She taught me how, back when we were in junior high."

He seems surprised. Perhaps he's remembering the girl he went steady with: virginal, naive, ignorant of sin.

"I never got hooked the way she did. Some failure in me, probably," she says, not altogether in jest. Once during a public demonstration a hypnotist summoned her to the stage but then dismissed her as a poor subject, and she'd felt inadequate.

Now they've reached the spot where Circle Drive diverges to the east from County Road. In their childhood Circle Drive didn't exist; Paul's house stands on what was then acres of marsh. Thirty-five years ago developers drained the land and trucked in tons of fill. From the evidence of mature trees and lawns, you'd never guess that cattails and skunkweed flourished there in living memory. Edie has heard, however, that basements in the development are notoriously damp. She thinks of Paul's aircraft, the tires awash in puddles in the spring.

He pauses, seemingly reluctant to leave her, and asks how long she'll be staying.

"Only a few more days."

"Maybe we'll run into each other again."

"There's the family party at Georgine's on Sunday."

"I doubt Arlene will feel up to it. She doesn't have much to do with the cousins, anyway."

"Monday I'm on my way back to Chicago."

"Yes, well." He stares at the thatch of scrub trees where County Road takes a gradual turn ahead of them, as though gathering himself to say something more, but then switches the tightly rolled magazine to his other hand and hurriedly crosses the road.

March, 1963. Out on Circle Drive the basement was dug, the house framed and the drywall and plumbing installed, but the day little Debra Jean was born the house still sat forlornly in a muddy wasteland, unfinished, while the contractor busied himself with another project at the opposite end of the county. So Arlene and Paul brought their firstborn home to the shabby duplex on Fourth Street where they'd been living since they got married. The duplexes had been hurriedly thrown up after the war as temporary housing for returning veterans. Eyesores, from the beginning. Still, better than being under your mother's roof, Edie guessed, or your mother-in-law's.

She rang the buzzer and waited on the low brick stoop, holding a box wrapped in white tissue paper. When Arlene opened the door, she had the baby over her shoulder and a cigarette in the other hand. She'd become a blonde as well as a mother since Edie had seen her last. "Edie," she said. "What a surprise."

Not exactly, Edie thought; the news must have reached Arlene that Edie was in town on an extended visit to her mother, without her husband. What Arlene meant was, she hadn't expected her cousin to show up on her doorstep. They'd barely exchanged a word in six years.

"Come on in," Arlene said. "The place is a mess."

She wasn't kidding. A card table held breakfast dishes, as well as old copies of *Family Circle* and piles of mail. Clothes hung from chair backs. On the couch were a mound of unfolded gauze diapers, a rumpled newspaper, a box of Nabisco chocolate chip cookies. Edie was not particularly taken aback that Arlene would live in this squalor, but she wondered how Paul could stand it

"Meet Debra," Arlene said, moving the baby from her shoulder to the crook of her arm. The child had a pink oval face and gray eyes, which seemed to study Edie with grave concentration. "Four weeks old. She smiled for the first time yesterday. Smile for Edie, Debra." But Debra remained solemnly thoughtful.

"I brought her something," Edie said.

"Drop your coat somewhere. Shove those newspapers on the floor and have a seat. Here, do you want to hold her?"

The next thing Edie knew she had a baby in her lap, and the flannel blanket that had been wrapped around the child was unwinding and spilling out wiggly arms and legs. Perhaps sensing she was in the hands of an incompetent, Debra wrinkled her forehead.

Arlene parked her cigarette, tore off the tissue paper from the box and opened it. She lifted out a delicate little white gown, hand-smocked and trimmed in lace. Edie had bought it at Marshall Field the day after her mother telephoned to tell her of the birth, two days after Si finished packing his things and moved out of the apartment. She'd spent an hour or more in the infant department, mulling over possible gifts. Why had she gone to so much trouble? She didn't know herself.

"It's gorgeous, Edie. Really."

"I guess she'll grow out of it pretty fast—not like a doll."

Edie remembered, and maybe Arlene did too, the time Arlene administered a haircut to Edie's best doll, the bisque one with real hair her grandmother had given her. The child punished for the crime was Edie.

"No, they definitely aren't like dolls. Dolls sleep at night." Arlene brushed ash from the front of her wrinkled blue duster. She'd gained weight with the pregnancy; something about her face looked flaccid. Edie thought she seemed oddly tense, maybe embarrassed for her cousin to see her this way—no makeup, bleached hair brown at the roots. "You'll find out what it's like," Arlene said, "one of these days."

"I don't know." The baby had turned her face toward Edie's sweater and was making gentle suckling sounds. She patted the child's surprisingly solid body. All at once Edie felt on the edge of tears. "I'm getting divorced," she said, although revealing this to Arlene was the last thing she could have imagined herself doing when she'd stood on the ugly brick stoop. She hadn't even told her mother yet.

"Oh, shit." Arlene picked the cigarette stub out of the ashtray and took one last drag off it. "What went wrong?"

To her chagrin, tears were trickling down Edie's cheeks. One dripped from her chin onto the baby's flannel blanket.

"Use one of those diapers," Arlene said.

"Si knew everything about everything." She snuffled into the cloth. It smelled like cold sunshine; Arlene must have hung the diapers on a line outdoors. "He was always right. No matter what, he wouldn't give an inch."

"He's probably a sonofabitch," Arlene said, lighting another cigarette, "and good riddance to him. But you have to admit, you can dig in your heels yourself. Talk about stubborn . . ."

Incredulous, Edie stared at her cousin. Her whole life she'd done nothing but knuckle under to Arlene's whims. Who was *she* to say—

"The rough time you gave Paul, for instance."

"You're not going to blame *me* for that, are you?"

"You acted like an idiot. Cut off your nose to spite your face."

"I can't believe I'm hearing this from you, of all people."

Arlene made a scornful sound in her throat. "That night at the reservoir wasn't something I planned or even wanted. It just happened."

"Well, things came out all right for you in the end, didn't they?"

Arlene took a drag from her cigarette and said nothing.

Paul and Arlene turn up at Georgine's after all, already seated in the living room with drinks in their hands, when Edie and her mother arrive after church. Arlene has made an effort. She's fixed her hair in a French twist and put on a dress that Edie remembers from perhaps twenty years ago, a constructed beige crepe that's much too formal for this gathering. On Arlene's scrawny body the dress looks as if it belongs to someone else. Those who haven't come from church—and that's almost everybody—are wearing slacks or jeans. Arlene doesn't seem to notice that people are trying hard not to stare at her. As Edie sips her white wine, her eyes, too, keep returning to Arlene's chest, as if the multiplying tumors inside have some supernatural magnetic power. A cigarette smolders in the ashtray on the arm of Arlene's chair.

Arlene is talking with feverish energy about the absurd mismanaged school system, the outrageous property taxes, how the town has given up and turned everything over to assholes who don't give a shit about tradition, such as the Memorial Day parade, which wasn't held this year for the first time ever. "Things were a damn sight better in the old days," Arlene proclaims.

Abruptly her eyes focus on Edie over by the cheese ball. "You agree with me, don't you, Edie?" she shouts. "You, at least, understand what I'm talking about."

Edie is tempted to ask *which* old days, precisely, she has in mind, but knows enough to keep her mouth shut. With Arlene you never win. Georgine's husband, Bill, freshens Arlene's scotch and soda, though from across the room Paul is shaking his head at her. She ignores him.

Most of the younger family members disappear into the den to watch a football game; the little kids put on their coats and run around outside on the frozen lawn. Compulsively Edie digs into the cheese ball. Paul's face is flushed. Now Edie can see why he thought— or hoped, rather—that they wouldn't be coming to Georgine's. It must have been Arlene's idea to make an appearance, to prove there was life in the old girl yet.

Somehow Arlene has shifted to the topic of hotshot lawyers and their ilk, bottom-feeders, growing fat on other peoples' misfortune. Remarks aimed by not-so-subtle indirection at Edie, she has no doubt. Edie who isn't dying of cancer, who escaped the disappointments of parenthood, who doesn't have an airplane—an *airplane,* for heaven's sake—absurdly landlocked in her basement. "You can't trust a damn soul these days," Arlene says.

Edie will not stay another second in this room. She carries her glass out to the kitchen to see if she can help with setting up the potluck buffet, but no one's out here, and she doesn't know where to begin with the jumble of foil-covered casseroles that fill the counters. Some of them must need heating up, but which ones? In the oven or in the microwave? Suddenly tired, Edie decides to leave these complicated decisions to others.

How glad she'll be to be back in her own cozy apartment, to collect her cat and water her plants and listen to the messages on her answering machine, to resume her life.

From an open bottle next to the sink Edie pours more wine into her glass, then stands looking out at Bill and Georgine's backyard. Some years back they converted their garage into an apartment for

Georgine's sister, who had early Alzheimer's, and Georgine was nanny and nurse for Millie until she finally died. The garage still has pink ruffled curtains in the windows.

Behind her she hears someone enter the kitchen. It's Paul, who must also have been driven to bolt. "What do they do with the apartment now?" she asks, to have something to say. "Since Millie died." And then she realizes how clumsy, how close to the bone, the question was.

Paul says, "They rented it for a while. But there was some problem with the tenant, I don't remember what." He too pours himself a drink from one of the clutter of bottles, an orange soda. "I'm sure," he goes on, "they'd be more than glad to have you, if you wanted to live there."

"Me?"

"I thought you might be contemplating retiring, coming back home to live." Standing next to her, he digs out a couple of cubes from a tray of melting ice and drops them into his glass. "I can understand why you wouldn't want to move in with your mother. You're so independent."

Is she? He seems to perceive some Edie other than the one she sees in her own mirror. "I don't think it would work, Paul. Coming back, I mean."

"Why not?"

"I've been away too long."

From the den come shouts—the Jets must have scored. The kids, in the backyard now, are throwing heaps of fallen leaves at each other. On the other side of the fence the neighbor's dog barks furiously.

She turns from the kitchen window to look at Paul. His face is worn, exhausted. "She's not this bad all the time," he says. "It's the scotch. There's no fat on her to absorb it, and it goes right to her head." He sets his glass of soda on the counter.

"You hardly need to apologize for Arlene—not to me."

"I saw the way you looked when you left the room. I hope you won't go back to Chicago still angry at her."

Arlene might die before Edie's anger cools, is what Paul means. It would be a sort of curse on both cousins, alive or dead.

"Blood is thicker than water, Paul. I know that better than anyone."

In an awkward stooping rush he takes her face between his hands and kisses her. His hands feel cold, and their grip is hard. Then he lets go. A moment later Georgine bustles into the kitchen and is giving Edie instructions about setting out the paper plates on the dining table, the plastic forks, the trivets and napkins and serving spoons. Even before the food is heated and everyone's loading their plates, Paul has helped Arlene out to the car and taken her home.

"You won't see her again," Edie's mother says to her daughter.

But it's not going to be that easy to kill her off, Edie thinks. In her own way, Arlene might actually turn out to be immortal.

THE SCOW

I hold in my hand two metal disks. Each has a seven-digit number stamped on one side and a hole drilled in the edge. Dulled with corrosion or ash, they look as if they have passed through fire, and I guess that's true. Gritty dust rubs off on my fingers.

This is what's left of them. My parents: John and Ella Hopkin, longtime residents of 23 Hillside Terrace, Brookfield, New Jersey, dead and gone these thirty years.

In some ways, it's fitting that these humble pieces of metal, which I've come upon in a box of odds and ends in my desk, are almost the only physical remnants of their lives. They would have disapproved of gravestones, resisted the idea of brass plaques. They disliked fuss, both of them.

Their reticence was partly on account of their upbringing: You don't whine in public, nor do you exult. Even within the family you don't speak of pain. Or grief.

But it's also a fact that they reached adulthood during the Depression, when people had to hoard every resource. For my parents, I think, the habit of thrift somehow came to include their store of feelings. Even if they had been religious, the concept of a funeral, especially one involving a casket surrounded by weeping mourners, would have struck them as profligate, both of money and of emotional energy.

That's why they joined the burial society, the function of which was to deal with a dead body as cheaply and expeditiously as possible—in their case, by cremation. They didn't consult with me, their only child, about this decision: They probably assumed that what was going to happen to their earthly remains was none of my business. At the time they signed up with the society they were actuarially far from death, and I was absorbed in gestating my first child. Even if they'd informed me, I doubt I would have given their decision a second thought.

But lives do not always conform to actuarial tables. One Sunday afternoon not many years later, as I was folding clothes in the laundry room, the phone rang in the kitchen. "Something happened to your mother," Dad said.

"What? What happened?"

"She fell down the cellar steps."

In my mind's eye I saw those steps. Narrow, splintered, cluttered with muddy work boots and cans of bent nails, saved from total darkness by a single 25-watt bulb.

I gripped the edge of the counter. "Is she going to be all right?"

"No, Franny. She's gone."

Gone? Just like that?

There would be no funeral, my dad told me. No memorial service, either. "That's the way she wanted it."

Before her body was cold, practically, the burial society spirited it off.

Two weeks later, when Carl had returned from a business trip and could mind the kids, I drove down to New Jersey, to the house I'd grown up in—the five-room bungalow that my parents paid four thousand dollars for in 1939. All over again I was surprised at how small and cramped and jam-packed the rooms were. And how frigid, since the thermostat was invariably set at sixty-two degrees.

At my dad's request I went through Mom's jewelry, choosing a few pieces to keep, and bagged up her clothes to give away. What set me to weeping was a cotton housecoat, red piping on the collar and cuffs, geraniums faded to pink, a rip in the threadbare cloth below the pocket mended with tiny even stitches. In one of the earliest photos of me my mother wears that housecoat. I am a naked, bemused, round-faced infant; she is girlish, even pretty. I considered cutting off the square red buttons and saving them to sew on another garment, but taking scissors to the housecoat seemed too violent an act. Maybe some customer of the Salvation Army would do it. I couldn't. I folded the housecoat into the plastic garbage bag with everything else.

For dinner I made fish chowder, my father's favorite. As I stood stirring the chowder so it wouldn't stick to the bottom of the dented old kettle, my father looked into the pot. At my elbow he gave off a strong odor of pipe tobacco, shreds of which adhered to his plaid wool shirt, and bay rum. Maybe, I thought, he was comparing the thickness of the chowder to my mother's. Suddenly, clumsily, he embraced me. "Oh, Franny," he said with a croak. Then he let me go and blew his nose hard. Even now, three decades later, I can't eat fish chowder without experiencing again that brief moment when my father revealed to me his sorrow.

It took some courage to ask him what had become of my mother's ashes. He might well have told the burial society to dispose of them as they saw fit.

"Hall closet shelf," he answered.

I tried to talk him into a little private ceremony. "You and I can go somewhere nice, and scatter them," I said. "Like the duck pond." Maybe read a few poems. Ever since I could remember there'd been a volume of Edna St. Vincent Millay in the front-room bookcase.

My dad looked at me as if I'd lost my mind. "The *duck* pond?"

To be sure, in the years since I'd graduated from high school and left home the duck pond had become encroached upon by an industrial park composed of prefab metal structures and the new multipurpose municipal building, also prefab.

"Well, you choose a spot, then."

He just shrugged. In the end, I had to return to Belmont without having managed any kind of ceremony to memorialize my mother.

The following February, on a Sunday morning almost exactly a year after her death, my father's car slid into a concrete barrier next to road construction on Route 4. Uncharacteristically, he wasn't wearing a seat belt, and according to the state trooper who called to give me the news, he'd been doing at least seventy when the car hit the black ice. "Route 4?" I said to Carl after I hung up. An endless strip of crummy stores some distance from where my dad lived: discount warehouses with names like Crazy Harry's, muffler shops, unfinished-furniture outlets. "What could he have needed so desperately?" I wailed. "On Route 4? On a Sunday morning?"

Once again, no body for me to grieve over. Once again, "No public service, at his request"—a request spelled out in the terse obituary he'd written for himself and deposited with the burial society. All that remained for me to do was empty out the house so it could be sold.

Because of the kids, I couldn't just take off on a moment's notice. And I admit I wasn't eager to face the accumulation of my parents' thirty years in that house. So it was June before I finally went down to do the job.

Before I left Belmont, I'd ordered up by phone a dumpster from a local waste disposal company. "The biggest one you've got," I'd said to the woman down in Hackensack, on the other end of the line. Sure enough, there it sat, plonked in the driveway next to the house, a veritable scow that might just have returned from a garbage-dumping voyage to Malaysia, a scabrous insult to the eye in this modestly respectable suburban neighborhood. On tiptoes I peered over the side. The rusted interior was empty except for some sodden sheaves of newspaper.

With the key that I took from the fake rock beside the stoop, I unlocked the kitchen door. The house, which had been closed up for four months, smelled of mold, pipe smoke, and something vaguely sweet and rotten, as though a piece of fruit had fallen behind the refrigerator. My shoes stuck to dirty linoleum.

I got down a glass from the cupboard and turned on the tap. Brackish water sputtered from the faucet. Hoping for root beer or ginger ale, I looked inside the refrigerator. Nothing like that. All the real perishables were gone, too, probably disposed of by the next-door neighbors, who also had access to the key so they could keep an eye on the place. What remained were pickles and mustard, a can of Maxwell House, the jar of gourmet strawberry preserves I'd given him for

Christmas. I unscrewed the lid. One teaspoon scooped out, the rest crystallized. Didn't he like it? Or had he only just opened it before the accident? My eyes began to tear.

That night, after a supper of freezer-burned toast and peanut butter and a shot of my dad's Canadian Club, I slept in my own childhood bed. The sheets that I'd taken from the linen closet still gave off the scent of Sweetheart soap, the oval cakes of which my mother used to remove from their boxes and leave as fresheners on the shelves. I wasn't sure that brand of soap was on the market anymore.

Sometime during the night I was awakened by thunder. Rain crashed against the window glass. I remembered the summer when cracks appeared in my bedroom ceiling and rainwater dripped onto the rug, and when my father climbed a ladder to patch the shingles, he slipped off the roof and scared the wits out of me (and probably my mother too although she didn't show it) but by a miracle broke no bones.

I remembered how my cat Timmy used to hide under my bed during thunderstorms, imagining he could keep himself safe that way. I realized I had never slept alone in this house before.

The next morning I stood at the kitchen counter and ate more toast, this time with my dad's hard-as-rock preserves instead of peanut butter. I gazed out at the backyard, in which knee-high grass grew, gone to seed. Because all spring I'd kept saying to Carl, "next week I'll try to go down," or "definitely, the week after," we'd never hired someone to keep the lawn mowed. At the rear of the yard, beneath some dejected rose of Sharon bushes, were stacks of windows that my dad scavenged some years back, when they tore down the old town hall. He'd talked about maybe building a greenhouse when he retired. At first the windows had been covered by a tarp, but it must have blown off in a storm. Some of the panes were broken, and dandelions sprouted through the gaps in the glass.

Depression Mentality, I've heard it called, the pathological impulse to accumulate bargains and freebies, linked with the inability to throw anything away. Nobody suffered from the disorder worse than my parents. You don't replace something perfectly serviceable simply because it's unattractive or not in the best condition, and when it breaks down or falls apart altogether, you put it in the cellar, because you might get around to fixing it sometime. You never know when that piece of scrap plywood or odd-sized pan lid will come in handy. In some ways I sympathized. They'd lived through lean years. His ambitions for higher education thwarted, my father took a low-paying clerical job after high school, and perhaps out of discouragement, he remained stuck in it. My mother earned pin money by doing demeaning little tasks like running up the costumes for a neighbor child's dance recital on her balky old Singer. Their nutty ways had roots in genuine experience.

I was determined, however, not to take on the burden of their possessions. This was 1970, when I and my contemporaries believed in traveling light, gathering no moss. Even the husband and two kids I'd acquired seemed like considerable baggage to my college roommates, one of whom was a photojournalist, constantly on the road, and the other a foreign service officer stationed in Istanbul. Hence the dumpster in the driveway, hence my plan to make a quick, surgical strike. I would allot no more than three days to this operation.

Since I was standing in the kitchen, toast in hand, I decided to start right there. I began to pull things out of cupboards and separate them into two piles: (1) the cookware and appliances destined for the Salvation Army and (2) the useless junk that no one could possibly want. The latter pile quickly became the largest. By nine o'clock the temperature in the house was in the high humid eighties; my parents had never seen the need for air conditioners. A hot breeze, laden with grass pollen, moved the café curtains in the open window. As I worked I occasionally became aware of the strange sweet-rotten odor I'd noticed the day before. The smell wasn't exactly unpleasant. Mystifying is more the word. For company I tried to tune in WQXR on my mother's counter top radio. All I could get without static was mindless jabber on WOR.

Devoutly I wished I had not ventured upon this job alone. I

should have left the kids with friends and dragged Carl down here to help. At least he would have been somebody to laugh with over the insane objects I found squirreled away in the backs of drawers: bundles of milk bottle wires from the forties; thousands of rubber bands; half clothespins missing their springs; bags and bags of rags; those little plastic covers like shower caps that my mother once put over dishes of leftovers, now disintegrating and useless; partly burnt birthday candles and pencil stubs and ballpoint pens that no longer wrote. I emptied shelves full of ugly, mismatched china, mostly the former possessions of various deceased relatives, gadgets that no longer worked, washed mayonnaise jars, and on and on and on. Part of me felt the fascination of an archaeologist in this midden heap, this palpable record of the domestic culture of the early twentieth century. A bigger part of me felt disgust at my parents' insecurity, their compulsive need to save all this rubbish against some future disaster.

The discards I carried out to the scow, many armloads full, and pitched over the side. I cringed as crockery smashed against metal. I felt especially bad about a set my mother had served iced tea in: tall blue-green china mugs with wooden handles, and a matching pitcher. Maybe they'd been a wedding present. However, only one mug remained intact, and the pitcher's lip was chipped and a black fissure ran up the side. I didn't enjoy throwing them away, but I couldn't rescue every single object to which some memory still clung, could I?

"Oh, she *was* hard," you might well say about my twenty-eight-year-old self. To be honest, I'd do the job differently now.

Next I attacked the front room. All the furniture, and there was a lot of it for a room that measured no more than twelve by fourteen, would go to the Salvation Army. Into the scow went my father's collection of stinking pipes, a hassock from which kapok had begun to emerge, a cheaply framed print of Van Gogh's sunflowers whose removal left behind a bright rectangle of lords and ladies and feathery trees and horse-drawn carriages on the otherwise faded beige wallpaper, and a floor lamp that had worked only iffily, something wrong with its wiring. I think the lamp was one of the furnishings my parents took possession of when my grandmother died, or perhaps a great uncle had passed it on to them.

Picking through the books, I opened the volume of Millay poems. It had never occurred to me to look inside it before, although as a child I was a great reader. Maybe the old-fashioned binding put me off, or the fact that it was wedged between *A Study of History* by Toynbee and *Decline of the West*. Ella Alice Field—my mother's maiden name—and the date 1928 were written inside the cover in fading green ink, in a more florid and flowing style than she later used, but recognizably her handwriting. She would have been eighteen.

I riffled through the pages and found a stanza my mother had underlined in the same green ink:

> *My candle burns at both ends;*
> *It will not last the night;*
> *But, ah, my foes, and, oh, my friends—*
> *It gives a lovely light.*

I was startled at the thought of my practical, tightlipped mother contemplating burning one's candle at both ends. But that had been in her youth, before the Depression and marriage to my dad. I closed the book and put it in the pile for the town library.

In the afternoon, the next-door neighbor, Mrs. Haas, still in her church dress, came to the kitchen door bearing a smallish square box. "We're awful sorry about your dad," she said. I wondered if she realized she was, in fact, holding his earthly remains. When the box from the burial society was delivered she'd signed for it and kept it for my arrival.

"So unfortunate," she continued, "those two terrible accidents, one right after the other. You never know what life has in store, do you?"

"No, you never do."

Mrs. Haas was a woman in her late sixties whose passion in life, according to my mother, was raising funds to have stray cats neutered and placed in good homes. Since she and her husband had bought the house after I'd grown up and left, I didn't know them very well.

"Lovely people, your mom and dad." Mrs. Haas glanced behind her at the scow, out of which protruded my grandmother's lamp, the shade drunkenly atilt. "Kept to themselves pretty much," Mrs. Haas said, "not that there's anything wrong with that."

I thanked her and took the box.

"Too bad there wasn't some kind of a service. Seems like there's something missing when there isn't a service."

Sweat trickled down my back, under my T-shirt. "Well, that's how they wanted it."

"You have to let people do things their own way, don't you."

Even when what they insist on doing is wrong-headed, Mrs. Haas meant, but was tactful enough not to say. She looked worried. In her mind was, perhaps, the idea that if you haven't had a funeral, God might not notice that you had died, and you could find yourself drifting in Limbo for the rest of eternity. I wasn't sure that I didn't, on some level, suspect the same thing myself.

Mrs. Haas urged me to call on her if I needed anything, anything at all, and turned and stepped off the stoop. Through the screen door I watched her give the scow a wide berth, averting her eyes from the jumble inside, and then cut through a break in the scraggly hedge.

Even with all the windows open, and an electric fan turning fitfully in the dining room window, the curious sweet-rotten smell persisted. Wearily I went out to my car and retrieved the flashlight from the glove compartment. I climbed up onto the kitchen counter and shone it behind the refrigerator, but all I found was dust.

The final room was my parents' bedroom. It was as my father left it that February morning when he took it into his head to drive to Route 4. Blinds shut, closet door slightly ajar, a pair of suspenders dangling from the knob. The covers on his side of the bed were turned back, narrowly; my mother's side remained smoothly tucked in. Sleeping alone, he hadn't moved his body into her space, not so much as an inch. I wasn't sure what to make of his reticence. Did it convey the continuing presence for him of my mother's slight, knobby body, even in death? Or only the meagerness of his sense of self? Either way, the sight made me miserable. I bundled up the sour bedclothes and carried them out to the scow.

Frantic by now to get the ordeal over with, I dealt with the bedroom savagely, refusing to consider who might get some use out of those shoe trees or take pleasure in that tarnished tie clasp, whether any life was left in the dresser scarves or curtains. Everything got tossed. It pained me that so little in this room, this intimate room I'd almost never entered as a child, was worth saving. The pain was physical, like a blow to the chest.

Finally, in early evening, I telephoned Carl. "How's it going?" he asked.

My parents' daughter, I couldn't bring myself to complain. "Not too bad."

"Still think you'll be home Tuesday?" He'd taken two days off work, and the office was short-handed.

"There's the cellar, that's what I'm really dreading. And I have to go through the papers in Dad's desk." The fan on the windowsill began to clank ominously. "They're coming to take away the scow first thing Tuesday morning."

"Scow?"

How ecstatic I would be to see the last of that thing, and all of its depressing, hideous contents. I pictured myself on Tuesday, dancing a jig in the road as the scow rattled and groaned down Hillside Terrace.

"Take your time, Fran," Carl said. "Everything's under control here. By the way, I can't find any underwear for Chrissy. Does she have underwear?"

Numb with fatigue, I went into town for something to eat. After my slice of pizza I took the long way back, abandoning four cartons of books on the library steps, hastily, as if the boxes held litters of kittens. I drove around by the duck pond. Teenagers hung out on the bank, probably passing a joint. Green scum floated listlessly on the surface of the water. Nary a duck in sight.

The cellar was where my mother died. Tripped, no doubt, over some piece of junk on the steps, lost her balance, split open her skull on the cement floor. I hadn't been down there since her death, but now I had no choice.

I opened the door and switched on the light. The steps were bare now, perhaps cleared by my father, perhaps by the emergency crew. I paused at the top. I knew what awaited me: electric drills with frayed cords, defunct toasters and shavers and clocks and radios from many eras, cans of dried-out paint, used car batteries and stacks of tires, dozens of dusty Ball canning jars . . . And blood on the floor. I doubted that you could scrub blood out of rough concrete, not with a ton of elbow grease.

Elbow grease. I can't ever get all the grime off the woodwork, no matter how hard I rub. My mother tips the ammonia bottle into my bucket. The fumes make me feel like I'm going to faint. She tells me to quit whining and to use more elbow grease. Idle hands are the devil's tools, she says, not that she believes in the devil.

My mother believes in cod-liver oil, never mind that it makes me gag. She believes in woolen leggings, never mind that my friends all wear dresses to school and have bare legs in January and never once catch pneumonia, never mind that the wool itches like crazy, worse than poison ivy. She believes in shoes with good support (Mary Janes will make your arches fall, like London Bridge) and oat-meal for breakfast and whole-wheat bread because white bread makes your teeth rot and your complexion pasty and three big glasses of milk every day because otherwise you'll get rickets, and never ever Coke, if you drink Coke your teeth will rot *for sure* and fall right out of your head.

My father believes in getting your homework done before dinner in case you get a stomach ache afterward. He believes in riding your bike facing traffic so you can see what's about to hit you and veer off into the ditch. He believes in minding your *p*s and *q*s, minding your own business, minding what you say and do in public because your words and deeds might come back to haunt you.

Always afraid of what might happen, the both of them. Always trying to ward off disaster. And now look what did happen, in spite of all their worrying.

No blood at the bottom of the steps, or none that anyone could see in the puny light of a 25-watter.

I spent most of Monday hauling rubbish up those steps and pitching it over the side of the scow. Every once in a while, after a particularly loud crash, I'd notice Mr. or Mrs. Haas at an upstairs window in their house, staring down on me. They, too, had lived through the Depression. Perhaps they thought that my prodigal wastefulness was inviting the displeasure of God, even more troubling than my parents' unceremonial way of dying.

At half past four the Salvation Army truck arrived. I confess it was hard to watch some of the furniture carried out the door, like the bookcase my father made for me when I was five or six, which was first painted red and later yellow to match daisy wallpaper he put up in my room for my eleventh birthday. But mostly I was happy to see the stuff go.

Again I drove to town for a meal, but this time I didn't go by the duck pond. When I returned, I noticed that my grandmother's floor lamp was no longer in the scow.

The bottle of Canadian Club at my elbow, I sat in the middle of the empty front-room floor and began to go through the papers from Dad's desk. Ancient checkbooks, phone and electricity and gas company receipts from the fifties and sixties. Income tax records. Auto, homeowner's, life insurance policies. Letters and Christmas cards in packets kept together with rubber bands. Mortgage payment stubs going back to the beginning. They'd finally paid the mortgage off last year: I remembered my mother telling me that on the phone, a hint of satisfaction in her voice. It was a few weeks before she fell down the steps.

Then I came to a business-sized envelope addressed to my mother, with a return address from North Bergen Oncology Associates. I pulled out a letter typed on crisp bond paper. "This is to summarize the conversation held in my office on 11/18/68," the doctor wrote. "Liver biopsy confirms a diagnosis of hepatocellular carcinoma."

I knew enough from my one summer as a candy striper in the

county hospital to understand that "hepatocellular carcinoma" meant cancer. Some dreadful kind of cancer.

". . . At present no drugs are available to treat this condition. Surgery is a possibility in selected cases. Unfortunately, you do not fit that profile . . . We recommend that you continue palliative therapy under the care of your general practitioner . . ."

I couldn't believe it. My mother had shared this information with my father, but not with me. Private she certainly was, a person whose whole philosophy of life prevented her from complaining, yet she was dying of a vicious incurable disease and chose not tell her only child.

Did she suppose she was protecting me, or what?

Angrily I unscrewed the cap on the whisky bottle and took a big swallow.

Why hadn't they sought a second opinion? Or demanded aggressive surgery? Or explored experimental treatments?

But those options would have been expensive, would have called attention to themselves. I began to think of the cellar steps. How much better than an embarrassingly public wasting away would be a headlong leap onto cement. She'd spare my father, spare me, the sight of her gradual decay. Yes, I could believe it of her, the determination such an act would require.

And then I thought of my father's death, almost on the anniversary of hers. Sliding into a concrete wall, going very fast, not buckled in. An unlikely death for him, I'd believed that from the beginning. And, when I thought about it, so like my mother's: its true drama disguised, kept secret from emergency crews, police, coroners, me.

Secrets. I remembered the bloody gauze bundle I saw on the edge of the tub when I got up to pee one morning. I must have been six or seven. "What's that?" I asked, frightened, but my mother just took it away. I remembered the scary red rubber syringe I sometimes found on the toilet tank. For enemas? For other adult purposes I couldn't even guess at? Then there was the time my cat suddenly disappeared. "Where's Timmy?" I demanded to know. "Timmy was sick." "Couldn't the doctor fix him?" "No. Eat your egg."

Were my parents' deaths yet more evidence of their secretiveness, their timidity, their fear of life? Or had they instead, for one time only, when it really counted, looked fate square in the eye and taken control of it?

I got up and went into the dining room to call Carl. The phone sat on the floor now that the rickety wrought iron stand that had held it had gone off to the Salvation Army. I picked up the receiver and heard silence. For a moment I almost panicked. And then it came to me that the phone company had disconnected the line, just as I'd asked them to.

At 8 A.M. Tuesday morning Julio and Miguel from Total Waste Services of Hackensack maneuvered the scow onto a flatbed truck. Standing in the driveway, I watched it rumble down the street and disappear around the corner. I didn't feel ecstasy, or even relief, but rather a sort of dull unease. I rolled up my sleeping bag and stowed it in the car, with cartons of photos and some of my parents' personal effects and papers. A representative from Garden State Realty would look the place over later in the day, but I didn't need to wait for her. She'd let me know over the telephone what the house might sell for.

On the kitchen counter, side by side, remained the two small square boxes containing my parents' ashes. I carried them out into the backyard, along with the Swiss Army knife from my key ring, and knelt under the apple tree my father planted their first summer here. Dew seeped through the knees of my jeans as I slit open the tape sealing the boxes. Inside each was a plastic bag, wired shut at the neck, with a metal identification tag attached. I cut the tags off and stowed them in my pocket. Then, one at a time, I upended the bags and shook them, letting the breeze carry the ashes into wet, overgrown grass. I didn't say a prayer. I couldn't think of one that would accurately convey my feelings to a God they didn't believe in.

Even then, kneeling there in the backyard, I knew that I hadn't come anywhere close to getting rid of that scow. Its ghost would sail in my wake forever.

THE AMERICAN WIFE

"I read today that unborn babies spend most of their time dreaming."

Eric doesn't comment. He's paring slices from a block of bright orange cheddar, pulling the knife toward him with precise strokes.

"But what do they dream *about,* do you think? I mean, they've had no experience. When they're awake there's nothing to see in there but murk, so what can they see in their dreams?"

Eric arranges the cheese on pieces of white bread, then puts the bread on the wire cage that surrounds the gas fire. Because the top of the cage is narrow, he must hold them there. His fingers are long and pale.

"What bothers me the most," she goes on, "is that I'll never find out. For some reason that really bothers me."

A little melted cheese is dripping onto the wire and beginning to burn. He hands her one of the sandwiches. Though Catherine isn't hungry, she takes a bite. The texture of the cheese is grainy, like softened plastic.

"What else did you do today?" he asks mildly. He doesn't glance at the unmade bed or the heap of dirty clothes stuffed between the wardrobe and the wall, but the question makes her feel defensive all the same.

"I walked down to Lipton's. I bought some tomatoes."

He's pouring steaming water from the electric kettle into the teapot, which already contains a quarter inch of cold tea and three or four damp teabags. The launderette is on the way to Lipton's, but he refrains from pointing that out. Something about the angle of his neck as he bends over the teapot, or the way his bangs march straight across his forehead, reminds her suddenly of the way he looked at her when she was falling in love with him. She sees the composed self-sufficiency—made vulnerable, if you could find a way to take advantage of it, by shyness—that had attracted her first to England and then to Eric. "Eric," she says softly, but he doesn't pick up on her change of mood.

"Today I found a chap who's agreed to move into the vacant room," he says, pouring milk into his mug. The bottle is nearly empty; the scummy look of the bits of cream clinging to the inside of the glass make a sour bubble rise in her throat.

"Who?"

"He's Ghanaian, I think, or maybe Nigerian. A second-year student. The room would suit him, since it's on the ground floor."

"Don't they have stairs in Nigeria?"

"He uses a wheelchair."

"Great. Just what we need around here: one more poor soul."

"He's quite capable of caring for himself."

"I didn't mean that, Eric," she says, abashed. "I'm sure he is."

Eric takes a handkerchief out of his pocket, looks into it to find a clean spot, and resolutely blows his nose. "He's coming round with his things tomorrow. His name's William."

"William? That doesn't sound very African."

"He told me he was born in Manchester, actually."

"Doesn't that make him as English as you are?" she asks innocently, folding the uneaten part of her sandwich into a piece of tissue. She's not sure whether this is a way to save it or a way to dispose of it.

"I suppose so, if you want to be technical."

"Technically—my situation is even worse. At least he has a name. I'll still be 'Eric's American wife' long after I'm in my grave."

"Well, Catherine, I'm afraid I don't see anything so dreadful about that."

"I'm tired, really tired, of everybody treating me like a freak."

"Nobody treats you like a freak. You just imagine it."

"I should be grateful I'm not black," she says, tugging cautiously at the tissue to see whether the cheese has stuck to it. "I have to open my mouth before they know for sure I'm a freak."

Eric rinses his mug at the sink and then begins to stuff shirts and underwear and cotton skirts into a duffel bag. The hook of a bra catches for a second on the bag's zipper.

"I'll do it tomorrow," she says. "It was so windy when I went out."

"Doubtless it will be windy tomorrow as well." He pulls on his raincoat and chooses a law text to read in the launderette.

"Please don't go out, Eric. I'll do it tomorrow, even if there's a hurricane."

But he is gone. She moves the landlord's flowered draperies a few inches back from the window and watches Eric open the front gate and latch it behind him. As he walks away from the house she sees his hooked nose in profile. His raincoat is black and his purposeful, long-legged stride, bobbing slightly, makes her think of a sea bird. Catherine's baby moves gently inside her hard round belly, dreaming—of what? she wonders.

They met in January, a year before, on the train from Carlisle to Stranraer. She was crossing over to Ireland near the end of a tour of the British Isles, a college graduation present from her parents. She arrived early for the train, found an empty compartment in the second-class coach and spread out her belongings; he slid open the compartment door just as the train was pulling away from the platform. He made no apology for barging in on her. For a while, as the train trundled through the Scottish countryside in a scattering of snow, they pretended to be unaware of each other's presence. He read handwritten notes in a ring binder. She ate a ham sandwich in a stale roll she'd bought in the station buffet. Absently, without looking up from his notebook, he reached over his head to press the light switch. Nothing happened. A look of irritation crossed his thin face and he pressed the other switch on his side of the compartment. The light failed to go on.

For the first time he looked at her. "Would you mind?"

Smiling, she pressed both light switches on her side. Nothing.

He scowled and left the compartment; the rush of cold air from the corridor blew her sandwich paper to the floor. In a few moments he was back. "No light at all in the whole coach," he announced.

"Can't they fix it?"

He shrugged.

"Second-class passengers get out and push," she said.

"Excuse me?"

"That's what we used to say when we were riding around in somebody's jalopy. An old car. When it would stall," she explained, figuring from the blankness of his expression that he had no idea what she was talking about.

He crossed his legs. "Are you Canadian?" he asked politely.

"American."

He didn't have anything to say to that. They looked out at the low hills streaked with fresh snow, unnaturally bright in the twilight, and seemingly as unpopulated as the face of the moon except for a few gloomy sheep.

"Do they leave them out all night in the snow?"

She had interrupted some thought of his own. "The sheep? I don't know. I don't know anything at all about farms."

"You're a city person, then?"

He rubbed his beak of a nose with long fingers. "Yes."

"So am I."

He paused before he spoke. "What city is that?"

"Brookline, Massachusetts."

"I've heard of Brooklyn."

"No, that's in New York. Brook*line.*"

He was silent; once again she'd killed the conversation. The inside of the compartment was almost completely dark now, and the train so quiet there might have been no other passengers. She could hear his breathing, slightly bronchial. He didn't try to look out at the landscape, but he didn't seem to be asleep, either. She thought suddenly: What if he were to put a hand over my mouth and assault me? Things like that happen sometimes, you read about it in the newspapers. A diffident, repressed sort of man, up to then completely respectable, given an unexpected opportunity . . .

Then there were the lights of a town, and the train was in the station at Stranraer. He picked up her suitcase with his own.

"You're taking the ferry?" he asked.

"Yes."

They left the train. She followed as he moved quickly through the milling passengers, most of whom were apparently unsure of the way to the ferry slip. Here rain was falling instead of snow, and the wind off the sea felt bitter.

Inside a shed their suitcases were inspected for concealed weapons and bombs. Automatically he raised his arms for the body search.

"Do you make this trip often?" she asked, when they'd reached the covered ramp leading to the ferry.

"When I can," he said. "My fiancée lives in Belfast." He lifted his wrist to read his watch.

On the ferry he chose to sit on the lower deck, and she supposed she'd seen the last of him.

She cuts up a chicken on the little round bread board, no larger than a saucer. In Britain they leave the foot, minus the toes, on the end of the leg and the pinfeathers in the pope's nose, and sometimes the chicken tastes fishy because it's been fed on fish meal. The cold flesh is sallow and unhealthy looking, and the joints resist the landlord's knife, which is so dull she's practically tearing the bird apart. She is on the point of tears. She turns the faucet on hard to rinse the dismembered parts.

William wheels into the kitchen. She lets him reach to switch on the electric kettle because he's made it clear that he expects to do for himself, though she'd enjoy helping him. His presence brings home to her that she no longer feels a similar inclination to help Eric, to care for him in a wifely way. Eric doesn't give her any clues, she tells herself in her own defense. He is so silent. He doesn't tell her what he wants of her, not even in bed. If he goes to the launderette or shops for groceries at Lipton's, the effect is to make her feel guilty that he has to do his wife's work on top of all his studies. A wife who has not a thing else to do in the world but care for him, and somehow cannot.

Perhaps it's this cold house slowing down her blood, paralyzing her.

William drinks his tea black, but with plenty of sugar. His teeth are amazingly white, unlike Eric's, which are yellowish and show signs of neglected decay. When William laughs, he laughs out loud. He plans to be a barrister. He will look wonderful in a white wig, Catherine thinks.

Already, with William in the kitchen, she feels warmer and more cheerful. She drops a nob of butter into the landlord's, Mr. Lally's, tinny frying pan and lights the gas under it. "I took the bus today," she says, shaking out the match. "I went to the antique market."

"What did you buy?" His voice has an inflection that has something to do with Manchester, but not everything. A hybrid.

"I looked at a set of dessert spoons with blue stones set in the handles. You'd never find anything like that in the States for the price. I didn't buy them, though."

He holds his tea mug with both hands and looks at her quizzically over the rim.

"We hardly ever eat a real dessert. Eric likes the kind of sweet you carry around in your pocket until it has fuzz on it, in case you get a secret craving. Toffee."

The fat sputters as she begins to put the chicken parts in the pan.

"Besides," she goes on, "we don't live that kind of life, where you use dessert spoons."

"Eric won't be a student forever. Things will change."

"Will they ever." She laughs ruefully. She is thinking not only of the baby, though; in fact, she's not truly convinced of its existence yet. The more frightening thing is that her connection to Eric is so amorphous it must surely harden, and in some way that she is incapable of predicting.

"At heart, Eric is very responsible," William says.

She knows he's only trying to reassure her, but the prospect of a responsible life as a solicitor's wife seems even more dismal than cheese sandwiches heated to a sticky consistency on the gas fire cage.

"What I wanted was to live with Eric in his room, sort of inconspicuously, like a cat or even a hot water bottle. I didn't think beyond that." She turns a thigh with a fork. "I came after him," she confides. "I didn't leave him a whole lot of choice. I didn't dream I'd stick out so, his *American,* that I'd change his whole life just by perching on the edge of it."

"You wouldn't have been content to be on the edge for long."

"Maybe not. But when you come right down to it, I didn't so much change his life as disrupt it."

After a pause he asks, "Are you homesick?"

She turns from the stove and looks at him. It's a good guess, though if she misses something, it's not Brookline, Massachusetts, or anything so tangible.

"I am sometimes homesick for Ghana, though I've never seen it. Things happen to me here that make me think I must jolly well belong somewhere else. But I don't, you know. I would be even more of an oddity in Ghana."

"That's what your mother did to you when she gave birth to you on English soil."

"Are you afraid that's what you are going to do to your child, Catherine?"

"I didn't want to have it," she answers softly, turning over the last of the chicken pieces. "What you said about Eric is true; he's very responsible. He just couldn't understand why I wanted to kill it."

"The voice of an Ulster woman," he'd said to her, over a fried egg, "is like rivets being driven into the Titanic." The ferry had been late, tossed in a gale, and when the bus deposited the half-dozen weary passengers at York Street Station in the middle of the night, she and Eric shared a taxi to the same bed-and-breakfast on Botanic Avenue, near the university. For two days she didn't see him at all; they arose at different times and went about separate errands in Belfast. She learned his name, though, read his tiny handwriting in the register on the hall table and knew that he lived on Tillmouth Road in Newcastle-upon-Tyne. Then on Wednesday they arrived in the empty breakfast room at the same moment.

Catherine sat at her table for one by the window and looked out at a damp little courtyard, where a few brownish Christmas roses were making an effort to bloom. A table away, Eric opened his paper napkin. She thought: If anybody's going to say anything, let him be the first this time. She finished the small glass of orange drink at her place. Crystals of undissolved powder remained in the bottom.

The bed-and-breakfast lady bustled in with a plate for each of them. One fried egg, one triangle of fried bread, two sausages, a slice of gammon, and one half tomato, lukewarm in its wrinkled skin. Coffee for each, racks of humid toast, and loud pronouncements about the shocking weather and the shocking price of sausages, also the price of electricity, and would they kindly keep that in mind when they bathed. Catherine smiled and nodded, breaking into her egg. As the bed-and-breakfast lady departed, a hot wave of fried bread and pop music blasted into the breakfast room from the kitchen.

"The voice of an Ulster woman . . ." he said then, and the bitterness in the way he spoke made her suspect that he did not mean the bed-and-breakfast lady only. Perhaps he's had some kind of falling-out with his fiancée, she thought, her curiosity aroused.

"Will you be going back to England soon?" she asked.

"I haven't made up my mind." He seemed about to say something more, and then tore off a piece of toast instead.

She smiled encouragingly.

"I expect you have friends here," he said, changing the subject.

"No, I'm alone."

"Not many people do that, come to Belfast in January just to see the sights." He sawed a sausage in half and put part into his mouth.

"I often find that I do odd things. Without meaning to be odd, that is."

He looked at her across the plastic freesias on his table, chewing thoughtfully.

"They just come out that way."

He nodded. "Perhaps you are willing to take more risks than other people."

"Risks?"

"Leaving your own nest."

She wondered if he and his fiancée had disagreed over this very issue.

"My family moved six or seven times when I was a child. I must have picked up the talent for it, or the habit anyway," she said.

"A particularly American talent, it seems."

"I guess that's true."

He wiped his fingers carefully with his paper napkin. "I could show you round Belfast a bit, if you'd like."

When Eric returned to Newcastle on Sunday, Catherine went along. That is how she came to move into Mr. Lally's brick rowhouse in Tillmouth Road, with peeling bottle-green trim, twelve chimney pots on the roof, and a rubble-filled front yard slightly larger than a bath mat. The baby was conceived in June. In September they married.

"I never wanted it," she tells William. She is seated cross-legged before the gas fire in his room, a much neater room than hers and Eric's, no long hairs wound inside dust balls or grayish sticky sheets on the bed. She toasts first the backs of her hands and then the palms. "Bloody frigid weather."

"You mustn't say 'bloody.' Americans don't know what it means."

"I know exactly what it means."

"It's rude."

"Shit."

"Why are you in such a mood?"

"I can never get warm in this place. I am cold, and sick, and stuck."

"Go away out of the house, then."

"You sound just like Eric. 'Find yourself a job,' he says. There *are* no jobs, and even if there were, they wouldn't give them to me, and he knows it. It entertains him to see me beating my head against a brick wall."

"Catherine," William says, softly and reproachfully.

"I'm sorry."

She pulls away from the fire, which suddenly feels too hot. It has made red blotches on her arms. She moves so that her back is gently touching one of his legs in the wheelchair, but doesn't look at him. She wonders if he can feel her body. She doesn't know whether he has sensation in his legs; she's never dared to ask. The accident that crippled him is a forbidden topic, not because he's secretive, but because it's not in his nature to complain. She's ashamed of the shrillness she heard in her own voice.

"You'll feel better when the baby is born. It is a restless time, waiting. My sisters are the same."

She rubs her stinging, mottled arms. "Poor baby, with Eric's nose and my foul temper."

"Poor baby," he echoes. He lays his hand on her hair and begins to stroke it, as though she is the baby. After a few minutes she gets up to make tea because she knows she is teasing him—or they are teasing each other—and she doesn't want to add that to all her other sins.

Catherine stops at the tandoori take-away near the launderette. It's a tiny shop padded with quilted glossy materials like the inside of a cheap jewelry box. She's received a birthday check from her parents, the amount of which she hasn't revealed to Eric, and she orders too much food: mutton tikka, prawn bhuna, special mixed vegetable curry, and two kinds of stuffed paratha. While she waits, she watches a Western serial on the color television set mounted high in the corner behind the counter. She doesn't recognize the program or any of the actors. Perhaps, she thinks, the show was filmed in a London studio with British actors simulating American accents. For a moment she feels dislocated, almost dazed, but walking up Brighton Grove with the bag of hot greasy cartons in her arms, she recovers her wits. The wind blows toward her, carrying pinheads of sleet.

Rounding the corner onto Westgate Road, she passes the hospital where she was tested and examined and given a date for surgery, all that time of her morning sickness sour with argument. She was shaken by the fierceness of Eric's opposition to the abortion and by the moral reasoning he used to buttress his stand; in the end she couldn't find the courage to go ahead in spite of it. She didn't cancel the appointment, but didn't show up for it, either. When he came home from the law library to find her still in his room he made no comment. He inserted a cassette into his little portable tape recorder and they lay on the bed listening to a Bach flute sonata, their fingers linked, both of them worn out. For those moments on the bed the matter seemed resolved. But of course, that would have been too simple.

In the street a yellow Number 41 bus passes, nearly empty except for a young girl smoking on the upper deck. A street cleaner with his barrow and broom moves along the curb, picking up potato crisp packets and soft drink cans. Catherine walks gingerly to avoid slipping on the icy paving stones, but inside her the baby lurches suddenly—a nightmare?—and she nearly loses her balance. The street cleaner pauses to stare.

"Will you have a lager?" Eric asks. She's made it safely after all, she's unpacking the cartons of Indian food and setting them out on the fruit crate they use for a coffee table.

"Thanks," she says gratefully.

He opens a can of lager for her and slides the beer down the edge of the glass, remembering that she hates to drink through a head.

She finds, now that the food is all spread out, that she has no appetite at all. The special vegetable curry is made out of frozen beans and corn, and the mutton seems to have been boiled separately from the sauce and just slipped into it while she watched the television cowboys.

Eric has not said anything about the quantity of food, or the expense, or the fact that she's only playing with it, taking little doll-like nibbles out of a paratha. On the other hand, he doesn't say anything else, either.

"I know what you're thinking," she says finally.

"Oh, yes?"

"That I'm good at starting things, but not so good at finishing them."

He swallows, looks at his plate. They are squatting on either side of the crate, right next to the gas fire. The sleety rain rattles the window glass, so loose in its old rotting frame that the draft can be felt as far as the fire. She shivers, and the muscles in her neck tense.

"Perhaps you're right," he says at last. "Perhaps that's the reason you like William so much."

"What do you mean?"

"Since he's a cripple, you'll never have to deliver." His reasonable, lawyerly tone does not hide his disgust. "You can just walk away."

She opens her mouth to protest, but sees in the same instant a terrible justice in his remark. She takes a deep breath. "If you can say that, I don't see how you can love me. But love wasn't ever the issue between us, was it?"

"No?"

There is a dull film of congealed oil on the mutton dish now. The tiny shrimp seem to curl up tighter in their sauce.

"Love didn't enter into the argument over the abortion. You won your case on other grounds."

"If you call it winning," he says flatly.

"Well, at least," she says, her mouth so dry she can hardly force the words out, "at least you proved something to your Belfast girlfriend, and that's probably what you had in mind all along."

He stares at her. "*You* chose to come here, Catherine."

"Easy come, easy go." She laughs sarcastically. "That's my talent, isn't it?"

He hesitates and then says, "Are you going to leave, then?"

For a moment she believes he'll plead with her to stay, the way he pled for the baby, but he doesn't say anything more, and she leaves his question unanswered. She's beginning to scrape the plates into the bag from the take-away. She fits the half-full cartons into one another and drops them into the bag, too.

A Sense of Morality

In November of 1969, the month 250,000 antiwar demonstrators marched on Washington, Miles and I departed that city for good and moved into a beach cottage in a blue-collar town south of Boston. Mortgage-poor, unable to sell our Cleveland Park house for what it was worth, we were, to put it bluntly, broke. But for me the cottage was more than a cheap winter rental. I was desperate to get away from tear gas and slogan-shouting and head-bashing. The deserted seaside represented my private escape from the war.

The first Saturday after the move, old friends from graduate school days drove down from Newton to inspect our uncharacteristically eccentric digs. We ate mussels for dinner and drank a great deal of jug wine, which Miles inevitably referred to as "plonk," an expression he'd picked up in London the year he researched the Anti-Corn Law League. From behind an expanse of plate glass we looked out at the dark Atlantic. "You've done a Good Thing," Ned Warner pronounced euphorically, as we contemplated the languorous progression of an oil tanker heading north, glittering like a parcel of urban property that had somehow become detached from the mainland. With a gratified smile Miles tipped more plonk into Ned's glass.

Around midnight the Warners left for home and Miles and I went upstairs to bed. An hour or so later I was awakened by a pair of indistinct shapes bumping softly into cartons, groping in piles of as yet unstowed possessions.

"Miles," I said, nudging him, "there are people in the bedroom."

"It's only the Warners," he muttered, from the depths of his wine-befogged sleep.

"It can't be the Warners," I said. "The Warners have gone back to Newton."

Cutting the argument off right there, one of the shapes grabbed some part of Miles's body and yanked him out of bed. "Just give us the big bills," he said, putting to Miles's throat what we later learned was our own boning knife. "You can keep the change."

Breathlessly I began to explain that we didn't *have* any big bills; the Federal Home Loan Bank had it all. You can't get blood out of a turnip, I said. At the same time Miles was chattering he didn't know where his wallet might be, but he'd do his best to find it, and please for the love of God don't kill him. I could tell from the wild croak in his voice that Miles was taking this turn of events harder than I. However, I didn't have a boning knife nicking into my throat.

Thug Number One frog-marched Miles downstairs in search of the wallet and I was left with Thug Number Two, who so far hadn't said anything. "Miles never knows where his wallet is," I confided, hoping to abort any suspicions that we were holding out on them. "Or his keys. That's one of the things about Miles."

We could hear, downstairs, swear words out of Thug Number One as they stumbled around in the dark, and out of Miles, a sort of unhinged keening. I found my husband's lack of guts embarrassing. I jumped out of bed and switched on the light.

"Hey," Thug Number Two said, startled. But I began to hunt for the wallet among heaps of underwear, and he didn't try to stop me. He was a slight man, twenty at most, with dull hair and a complexion that looked like it had been conditioned with a cheese grater. He held my bread knife, the serrated kind, and on his hands were two of my oven mitts. "So we don't leave fingerprints," he explained, with a wave of one mitt.

"Good thinking."

"My cousin thought it up," he said modestly. "We cut your phone wires, too."

"The phone hasn't been hooked up yet."

"Oh."

An outraged shout came from below. "The wallet's got six fuck-ing bucks in it!"

I shrugged: I'd told them so.

After a moment's thought Thug Number Two asked, "You got any gold?"

"Only my wedding ring," I said untruthfully.

He stared, rather puzzled, at a tangle of necklaces on my dresser: strung apple seeds, African clay beads. It was becoming clear that nothing about us was what he and his cousin had expected. "Oh no," he said, "I wouldn't take your *wedding* ring."

In the next few days Miles's salt-stained wallet and three oven mitts washed up on the beach. The fourth must have gone out to sea. Weeks later, early on a Sunday morning, the police invited me down to the station to look at mug shots. "No," I told the captain finally, "none of them is the man I saw."

"Right," he said. "Now we're going to show you a bozo we picked up last night on another break-in."

For sure he wasn't the kindly acned thug who'd scrupled to take my wedding ring. This man had a day's growth of coarse black beard, and although he was subdued—there in the captain's office, hand-cuffed—I saw nothing modest in him. "Say something to the lady," the captain prodded, and the man spoke a word or two in a mumble.

I thought he might be Thug Number One, the man I'd heard but not seen. But I couldn't be sure. "Do you have a cousin?" I asked. "A person with problem skin?"

"Nah," he said, and so far as I know, the police didn't pursue the matter.

But I saw Thug Number Two once more. It was in the produce department of a Dorchester supermarket; he wore a stained bib apron and was taking acorn squash out of a crate. In the intervening years his complexion had not improved. He flushed, recognizing me, and I began to shake. I could have had him arrested on the spot, I suppose, but instead I wheeled my cart on by. Out of a sense of honor, or morality, he'd spared me my wedding ring. Since then, I myself had cast it aside.

RED WOMAN, BLACK WOMAN

The tour bus sounds its horn at each twist in the narrow road, but it never slows. We'd be dead before they heard, she thinks, without alarm. Philip sleeps beside her, his neck stretched and exposed, his gray hair moving a little in the wind. She is touched that he trusts her enough to let her see his exhaustion.

Greek air smells the way a clay pot does when you first pour water into it—at least it does on this island. By moonlight the olive trees look coated with dust, and oranges and lemons are ripe on the trees at Easter time.

They reach Lindos as the sky is lightening. In the Plateia there is a hushed sorting of baggage and then they are led up through a maze of cobbled streets to their self-catering villa on the hillside below the acropolis. The guide shows Philip how to change the gas cylinder in the stove and work the hot water heater. When he's gone, Amanda finds a bottle of white wine in the little marble kitchen. "Shall we uncork it?" She is charmed by the unexpected gift.

"It's too late for wine—or too early."

"Are you being poetic?"

"No, just tired. Come lie with me, Amanda." He pulls back flimsy cotton coverlets. Underneath, the sheets on the twin beds are damp and unaired.

"I want to look around. I can't just hop into bed without knowing where I am."

"Come soon."

The air is cool at this hour, and it seems to have a quality of tension, of anticipation, perhaps because the sun will soon turn it baking hot. She walks barefoot on the pebbled terrace. It is made of black and white beach stones set in the design of a long fish. From the sea below comes no sound, a slate-colored sea with no perceptible tide.

Amanda first becomes aware of the woman next door as she and Philip sit on their terrace eating lunch. The woman is wearing a red dress—or a sort of red, anyway. The color, Amanda thinks, might have been achieved by dyeing the material with berry juice and afterward fading it unevenly in sunlight. The woman stands on the flat roof of her cottage, holding a brush attached to a long pole. As Amanda peers down on her, the woman dunks the brush into the pail and then leans over the edge, her long ragged sleeves falling over her hands, and scrubs the wall down as far as she can reach. Her movements are intent, though clumsily inefficient. She makes Amanda think of a dog trying to scratch the back of its neck.

"What's she doing, Philip?"

He holds his round of bread with a slice of local cheese neatly balanced on it and considers. "Whitewashing."

"But she's turning the house grayer and grayer."

"Perhaps she's too poor to buy whitewash. Or possibly she has a bat in her belfry."

"Poor old thing."

"She looks happy enough."

It's true. The woman has finished wetting down all of the wall she can reach from the roof and stands now in her yard, scrubbing upwards. She is singing, or chanting rather, in a hoarse good-humored voice. Splashes of whitewash rain down on her jaunty round face and on the weeds and broken jugs in her yard, but she doesn't seem to mind.

Philip pours some wine and touches Amanda's arm with the cool glass. "How about paying some attention to me? Forget the crazy old woman."

"For some reason she interests me."

"I thought the point in coming here was to think about each other."

The wind has loosened Amanda's light brown hair. She tucks it up under her scarf and turns to look at the sea. In the cove the water is azure now, clear and shallow. A yacht with furled sails floats to the end of its anchor line and gently tugs. Several motor launches and dinghies buzz around it, shuttling people back and forth to the beach. "This sounds silly," she says, "but it hadn't occurred to me that there'd be all sorts of other life around. I imagined an empty, uncluttered place."

"There's no place in the world like that, Amanda."

She tosses the heel of the loaf to some small speckled birds that have landed on the terrace, scattering them. As usual, he's right. He knows a good deal more about the world than she does, despite the fact that she's nearly thirty-six and the former manager of a moderately successful gift shop on the coast of Connecticut. The sun is hot. Flies settle on olive pits in a saucer.

She remembers the treacherous drive between Rhodes and Lindos in the early hours of the morning, silvery dust on the leaves of the olive trees. Already the ride seems like a dream.

Leaving cheese rinds and cigarette butts and orange peels on the table, they go inside and lie together on Amanda's bed. As he fondles her breast Amanda sees, not for the first time, that his cheek sags on the pillow and his eyelids are shot through with hundreds of minute creases. Philip is over fifty. How much over she's not sure, although they have lived together in his London flat for the best part of a year, ever since they met in that city, acquaintances of acquaintances, and he persuaded her to let the tour return to the States without her. At the time she'd been too much in love, too flattered by the attention of this distinguished man, to care about his age, and now . . . Well, to ask would be awkward. After he is satisfied he pulls himself from her body, trailing a thin milky dribble across her thigh. Immediately he falls into sleep.

When they arise in the late afternoon, the woman in the red dress has disappeared and the house has dried bone-white. She *was* whitewashing, after all, Amanda thinks. How stupid of me. To worry that she didn't know what she was doing.

Their villa is on the donkey route. In the mornings and then in the late afternoons the guides lead alarmed-looking tourists, clumsily astraddle, up to the acropolis and down again. The guides moan at the donkeys, closemouthed, nasal: Whether they're expressing sympathy with the donkeys' lot or venting their own sorrows, Amanda isn't sure. No, she decides, the sounds are more like warnings to the animals. Don't stray, or attempt to resign. You clip the scrubby grass that grows between road and wall, I clip the tourist. Otherwise, no life for either of us.

Amanda and Philip talk about making the donkey trip up to the acropolis, where there are fortifications and, according to the guide-book, a couple of reconstructed temples. But one day it's too hot, they agree, and the next Philip begs off, a touch of indigestion from the taverna meal the evening before. After that, the guidebook remains unopened on the tile-topped coffee table, buried under a pile of hard-cover books that Philip brought with him on the plane, works on eco-nomics and diplomacy.

Hour after hour Amanda sits in a deck chair staring down at the village, as though she can force her brain to retain the images and store them up against some future personal famine: plastered white houses, jammed precariously wall-to-wall against the hillside, serene as eggs. At first the grapevines in the courtyards are dead stalks. Before her eyes, buds appear like parasitic growths and then unfold into flat transparent hands. Poppies bloom, straggling out of broken patches in the walls, delicate as puckered silk.

Because Philip's skin is fair and tends toward allergies, he prefers the shade. Frequently he lays aside the book he's reading and calls to her. When she moves out of the sun he is there to touch her, his grip uncomfortable sometimes, and to fasten her gaze with his own. "You'll grill out there," he says, making a joke out of it, "like a chicken on a spit." But his need for her is plain, and over the months they've been together that has come as a surprise to her.

She knows, from offhanded references his friends have made in her hearing, that he has been involved in numerous liaisons. Journalists are like that, she supposes, even those who write learnedly on international affairs for the *Times*. Accustomed to odd hours, prone to the accidental stroke of luck or ill-luck. She remembers the women at a party to which Philip took her soon after they met—enterprising, varnished, tough as gristle—and since she has little else to go on, Amanda identifies Philip's past lovers with those women. He must have had to be tough, too, protective of himself.

But he's different now, at least with Amanda. He seems to have fewer defenses than she first thought, and the discovery pleases her but is also somewhat confusing. She stands in the doorway of the villa peeling an orange and feels his fingers trace the length of her spine from vertebra to vertebra. He turns her head and kisses her mouth. Juice drips from her fingers onto marble paving.

"You like to kiss gently," he observes, puzzled. It's almost a reproach. Possibly, she thinks uneasily, he needs more from her than she knows how to give.

At six in the evening the woman in the red dress comes out of her cottage carrying a rusty can. She dips into the oil drum she uses as a rain barrel and splashes her face and arms. Circling away from the barrel in a shuffling bob and weave, she pours water from the can onto her hair and pats it down with her fingers. For a moment something in the street distracts her and she halts. Then, curiosity apparently satisfied, she returns to the barrel and repeats the whole busy ritual, the way a wasp, interrupted in nest-building, begins again from scratch. When she finishes, she returns the few drops of water that are left in the can to the oil drum. Then she closes the window shutters, moving aside the rocks that prop them open, and latches her door with rope and peg.

Amanda leans over the edge of the terrace, watching the woman scramble down a path between whitewashed villas, skipping from wall to wall to avoid the donkey dung.

Several days pass before Amanda realizes, to her considerable surprise, that a second old woman lives in the same one-room cottage. This one is dressed all in black. Her skirt drapes down to her ankles; a black kerchief covers her hair and is folded back again to cover her chin. Her eyes are tiny and sharp. Resolutely she pokes in the rubble in the yard with a stick as though she has lost something there and is determined to find it. With a broken-handled broom she sweeps out the cottage and wets the floor down with water from the oil drum. She hobbles between doorway and yard, shaking out bedding and emptying pans of swill into a ditch, doing her best to create order out of disorder.

The woman in black pays no more mind to Amanda than has the woman in red. Good, Amanda thinks, my staring won't embarrass them. But there is something insulting about their indifference, too— that she's of so little account. What she craved in London was a place so far away from Philip's disapproving or patronizing friends that no eyes pried. Now she finds it's disconcerting to be invisible.

Day by day she watches the black woman and the red woman alternate in the doorway of the cottage, like weather forecasters in a toy barometer. In the late afternoon, with the sun hanging over the western cliffs, the interior of their cottage is illuminated. Just inside the door is a painted chair with a rush seat. Through the window she sees a raised wooden platform where bedding is kept, a striped bolster rolled up and a purple wool coverlet spread out to air. On the wall hang plastic sacks, some clothing, and objects that might be cooking implements. The women come and go, wetting their hair and pouring water on the cement floor.

One window in the cottage overlooks the sea. The women could, if they wished, open its shutters to get a view of the beach, the abandoned windmills, the ruined pre-Hellenic tomb on the end of the northern claw of the harbor. But neither woman ever unhooks that latch, as far as Amanda can tell.

She wonders where they scuttle off to. Are they charwomen in one of the big villas? Are they fruit pickers? Or do they keep some more obscure appointment?

Down in the village market one morning, Philip stops to buy oranges for Amanda from a fruit seller who squats in the street. The old woman heaps the oranges on a scale. They have ripened on the trees; they still have stems and leaves attached. She balances them with lumps of brass and grins, toothless. "Two kilo, *ne?*" She is dressed all in black and her chin is bandaged like a nun's. "Very fine orange. *Orea.*"

Philip stuffs the oranges into a string bag he has purchased for the transport of groceries and pays the old woman. As they move away from her low mounds of fruit spread out on a cloth, shopkeepers selling pottery, embroidered shirts, bracelets, call after them. "Just have a look, M'sieu, Madame."

"Damn," Philip says, counting the coins in his hand. "The old witch shortchanged me."

"What can it be, a few pennies?"

"I don't enjoy being cheated, Amanda, even for a few pennies."

"She's one of the women who live next door, I'm almost certain."

He snorts. "Lindos is crawling with grannies in black. You're obsessed with those old women."

"It's the contrast between them that I find fascinating. The black one sane and sharp, the red one mad as a hatter."

"Let's drop the subject," he says. "Do you want to buy some *spanakopeta* for lunch?"

But they pass the shop without going in. Nettled at Philip's suggestion that she's becoming a bore about the old women, or that her interest in them is somehow unhealthy, she moves a few steps ahead of him. What else do he and I have to talk about, she asks herself bitterly, besides runs on the pound and the energy crisis?

It's mid-day: not a bit of shade on the road. She smells cumin, onions frying in oil, freshly cut leather sandals hanging outside shops, donkey dung. From behind villa doors come muted sounds. The inner gardens, carefully watered and planted with hibiscus, are shut away from them.

A gray tabby with a gash in its neck drops from a wall in their path and then bolts. The sea on her left is so bright it gives Amanda a headache to look at it. She glances back and sees Philip picking his way over the cobbles, his head lowered. The string bag of oranges thumps heavily against his leg. When he reaches her, she leans her face against his shirt and feels the warmth of it. "Darling, darling," she whispers.

After lunch Philip goes inside for a nap and she moves the deck chair to the edge of the terrace, scraping it over the pebbled floor. The sun is at her back. She sees the old red woman below, hanging out bits of wash on the bamboo staves that separate her yard from the villa behind. The woman pats down a square of cloth and then changes her mind and lays it upside-down on a place slightly farther along the fence. She swings about in small circles, her head nodding from side to side: a waltzing mouse.

She takes a brass pestle in her hand and does something with it on the platform between door and window, where Amanda can't see. Shaking her head, she circles with the pestle in the yard and then disappears again. Now she has half a lemon in her mouth. She sucks at it, shuffling in and out of the cottage, one hand on her hip. She eats the pulp and part of the skin, as well. Does she notice how sour it is? Amanda wonders.

Later, while Philip still sleeps, Amanda decides to walk back down to the village. Shopkeepers are beginning to crank up the metal guards they lowered over store fronts for the long afternoon siesta. Though it's past four, the heat remains oppressive. She browses in tourist shops among heaps of hand-painted tiles and plates and dusty copperware, thinking vaguely of buying some small thing to remember their holiday by.

In a dark shop at the end of the row she finds some worry beads, antique amber the color of butterscotch, hanging from nails on the rear wall. These were not made for tourists. Amanda fingers the smooth beads, picturing the kind and wise old men who owned them long ago. The proprietor slips up behind her. He smiles, twisting his silver ring. "You like?" he asks. "I give you special price." But she has no idea what the beads are worth or how to bargain. In her job back home she relied on fixed prices, agreements in writing. Surely she'll be taken, just as Philip was cheated by the fruit seller in the market. The shopkeeper is practically on top of her, his garlicky breath on her cheek, and suddenly he's all the men she's ever been with: the married tax lawyer whose baby she carried for three months before the abortion; the shy oculist who pleaded with her to let him do strange things to her body; the guy who sold mixers and attachments, dough hooks and shredders, and who, when she told him she wanted to break off with him, started filling her mailbox with deranged letters and postcards.

She pushes by the shopkeeper and runs out into the street. *Philip,* she thinks. She runs, slipping on the cobbles, up to the villa.

He is smoking, sitting on the edge of his bed. "I woke and found you gone."

"I was just walking."

"Don't *do* that to me, Amanda."

The sky is overcast, chalky, like *ouzo* mixed with water. The weather is going to turn. Down on the beach a bulldozer roars, scooping up the stones that winter storms have laid there and depositing them in an untidy pile. Perhaps the stones will be picked over, divided out by color and size, set into the terraces of new villas farther up the cliff. Or perhaps when no one is looking they will just gradually return to the sea.

As she fries chunks of lamb in a pan, Amanda becomes aware of the squabble. At first she thinks it's the speckled birds, flapping at each other over bread crumbs, under the noise of the bulldozer. Then she thinks a radio blares somewhere. No. It's the two old women in the yard below.

She lowers the flame under the pan and goes out to the terrace. The red woman stands swaying in her doorway. The black woman flies about, raising her arms as though to strike with a curse. Both are screaming, fierce and bitter. The red woman in her wild laryngitic voice yells, *"Ochi. Ochi."* No. She weeps into her drooping red sleeves. Finally, exhausted, she drags herself up to the bed platform and lies down, her bare feet drawn up to her body, the soles of them exposed to Amanda's gaze. The black woman mutters, reties her kerchief tight under her chin, sits on the rush chair in the doorway. Her shrewd eyes glitter. There is silence.

Amanda realizes that Philip is behind her. "Are you trying to guess what the fight was about?" he asks.

"No. I know."

"Do you?" His voice is calm, amused, a little condescending. He lays his hand on her shoulder.

"The cottage is too small. There isn't enough room in it for both of them."

"Who won?"

"No one can win, not until one of them drops."

Wondering whether it will rain, Amanda goes inside to finish cooking the dinner.

HIDE AND SEEK

1. 1957

Over at Nick's there's a fig tree. You couldn't call it a particularly vigorous tree. It spreads out as if it can't decide which of its trunks is strong enough to be the main one, and every summer, as if it's doing you a big favor, it produces a skimpy amount of sickeningly sweet, purplish fruit. The seeds feel gritty in your teeth. By October, Nick's grandfather has wrapped the tree in layers made of strips of sheet and sewn-together squares of burlap, tying the whole thing up with yards of string and twine. That's what you have to do if you're determined to grow a fig tree in this climate.

Nick's grandfather, Nonno, is a toothless old character who hobbles around in the garden planting or hoeing or digging up vegetables. He's forgotten what few words of English he ever knew, and his family never learned his language, except for Nick's father, who can say swear words in Italian. Nick looks like Nonno, and the both of them look like crows. Beaky noses, and hair shaggy on the neck, and eyes that gleam the way a crow's do when it spots something it wants to seize and carry to its nest.

This past summer was when we started the game. It's a variation on hide and seek, I guess, though the rules are confusing and have changed some from when it first began. Half the kids run around looking for the other half, and when they find them, corral them "home," a dead locust trunk that serves Nick's mother as a washline pole. Since I tend to daydream in my hiding place—such a clever spot, always, no one finds this boy for ages—who is on which side at any given time is usually a mystery to me.

All summer long the neighborhood kids bolted their suppers and gathered at Nick's, the perfect place for the game because there are dozens of good hiding places. Nick's house, which was built by Nonno himself, was there long before the woods and fields surrounding it were turned into developments. The property is huge. There's a tool shed and a potting shed and a decaying chicken coop that now shelters rats, a garage that used to be a barn, a grape arbor, a raspberry patch and clumps of gooseberry bushes, an apple orchard, a gigantic vegetable garden. Now that it's November the only thing left in the garden is cabbages, but until September there was corn, which we found excellent for hiding in.

The big old house is off limits, because Nick's mother draws a line at having the whole neighborhood tearing through it. If you sneak in through the back entry, though, you can get down into the cellar. It's a little creepy. Shelves and shelves of old-fashioned canning jars down there, covered with cobwebs. Nick's grandmother put them up, and she died before the war, before Nick and I were born. If you ate anything out of those jars you'd probably be poisoned. The floor is bedrock and fieldstone, and in wet seasons a stream runs between the stones right under the house. This always amazes me, because my own father is passionate to the point of mind-numbing boring about the importance of dry basements. To him a wet basement is like being in a boat with a deadly leak in the hull. To him a wet basement is a kind of sin.

One thing that makes the game exciting is Nonno's wrath. At any moment the old man is liable to jump out of a bush, threatening you with a hammer or a pickaxe and bellowing in Italian. Start saying your prayers if he catches you trampling one of his plants.

Even after school started we went on playing the game, even after Nick's grandfather bundled up the fig tree in preparation for winter. Then playing became more of a challenge, because of the possibility of crashing down the cellar steps in the dark, or being locked for hours in a frigid shed until somebody got around to rescuing you. Most of the kids, especially the younger ones, stay inside after supper now. Only a handful of diehards are left.

The truth is, I've gotten tired of the game. For one thing, it's pretty uncomfortable squatting in some cold, damp corner waiting for a searcher to stumble on you, more or less by accident. But things are iffy at home, and I don't much want to be there, either. My sister Marybeth's away at college. Since she left, the house seems quiet—too quiet. My father's apparently brooding over something, maybe having to do with his job. He's out of the house a lot. And my mother . . . I can't tell *what's* up with her. So every evening after supper I leave home, whether my homework's done or not, and run crazily around in the frosted grass at Nick's.

Tonight it's Sunday, school tomorrow, and only Nick and I are playing. He's IT. I'm hiding behind the potting shed, my boots in a pile of broken glass that's been here forever. The moon's nearly full, and something about the way it lights up the fig tree in its mummy wrappings makes me uneasy. Far away I can hear Nick calling: *Ready or not, here I come!*

Suddenly the fig tree looks like a patient in a hospital, limbs all bandaged up that way. The victim of some terrible freak accident. Or a person with body tumors so malignant the hospital workers have to be protected from the cruddy pus that's seeping out from the lesions under the bandages.

Nick calls: *Prepare yourself to meet your fate!*

I can't stay in this spot another moment, looking at that tree looming out of the dark. From Nick's voice I know he's somewhere near the barn, so I blast through the raspberry thicket, pause for breath a moment behind the tool shed, and then race across the lawn and up the steps to the back door of the house. Luckily, the bolt hasn't been slid across from inside.

Now I'm in the rear entry, the outside door shut behind me. My mouth is dry and my thumping heart makes my ribs feel sore. Dampness is rising from the cellar. I think I hear the trickle of the steam wending its way between the stones. No sounds come from the kitchen. The dishes must all be washed, dried, and put away and everybody watching television or in bed.

I think about my own house, a three-bedroom bungalow a few streets from here. It's got a one-car garage behind it and a fenced yard the size of a beach towel, as my mother says. Unlike Nick's, there's no good places to hide.

My mother's probably still sitting at the kitchen table, smoking. The way she looks has changed lately. She hasn't had her hair cut in a while, and it's dry and sort of blanched-looking. It falls around her face in uneven lengths, and the strands seemed frayed at the ends, like rope that has begun to unravel. I can see her there at the table, pushing her hair away from her face with her fingers. They're spread apart and held stiffly, full of tension.

During the summer she took up smoking again. For some reason that made my father furious, but she didn't pay any attention to all the things he said about how bad smoking was for you and on and on. She dug out an old Ronson she'd saved from when she used to smoke, before she married my dad, and even when she doesn't have a lit cigarette in her hand, she'll be holding that lighter.

In the movies, it happens all the time that married people fall in love with someone else. I think about my father with some other woman, like Mrs. Lubecker, who he kissed in our kitchen during a party, a couple of years ago. He didn't know I saw him, but I did. Maybe my mother has found out that he doesn't love her anymore and is pondering what to do about it. When she sits there in the kitchen, staring into space, rubbing her fingers over the smooth warm metal, she could be thinking about leaving him, leaving us. I hate my father, I decide.

Where the hell is Nick? Probably he's given up trying to find me and has gone in by the front door and is now doing his math homework. Stupid, standing here in the damp. But to get home I'll have to go past the fig tree.

I'm freezing. I feel like I've just been vomiting hard or somebody's been pummeling me in the gut. My eyes sting with salt and I'm shaking all over. I've got to get out of here, but I can't.

Now the cellar door opens. For some reason Nick doesn't yell *You're it* or *Game's over.* Maybe he doesn't know I'm here yet. Suddenly my throat makes a weird sound, as if I'm being strangled.

"Ryan?" he whispers. I can't answer.

I hear the door shut. The landing is narrow and the wooden steps down into the cellar treacherous. If you fell and landed on bedrock you'd probably break every bone in your body. Nick's right next to me. I'm shaking even more now, and tears are dripping from my chin onto Nick's jacket. I feel his arm and shoulder firmly against mine. It would be impossible for him not to realize something's wrong with me.

Nick doesn't say anything, though. His arms are around me. He holds me so tightly that after a while the shuddering stops, and I can open the back door and walk down the steps. The moon is behind a cloud bank. I don't even see the bandaged fig tree as I cross the lawn and leave by the gate. The rest of the way home is lit by streetlamps.

2. 1962

In a booth in a diner on the outskirts of the small city of Meecham, Nick and I sit drinking coffee. We've received permission from Father Pokorny, the assistant headmaster, to be taken out for the afternoon by a non-existent aunt of Nick's. Instead we changed into jeans behind the field house, rolled up our St. Bartholomew's Academy blazers and trousers and stuffed them into a duffel and stowed it there, hiked overland to the road, and hitched into Eatonville, the nearest town. There we caught a bus and rode through miles and miles of bleak February countryside.

The diner, just off the highway, also serves as Meecham's bus terminal, its link to the outside world. Its name is the Crown. At the Crown, aside from Burgers Fit For A King, you can buy gasoline, ashtrays in the shape of toilets, cold beer in sixpacks, flyspecked road maps, and Rolaids. This is where the bus unceremoniously dumped us.

From the pocket of his leather jacket Nick produces a slip of paper, which was originally inside a fortune cookie. *You have an unusually magnetic personality,* it reads in faint red type. On the other side is a phone number written in ball-point. "You want to make the call?" Nick asks. "Or shall I?"

"Be my guest."

Nick slides out of the booth and walks with studied casualness to the pay phone on the wall next to the Gents. He deposits a coin and then dials the number, reading it off from the back of the fortune. After a while Nick speaks a sentence or two and then appears to be listening to some lengthy explanation or instruction at the other end. Finally he nods and says a few more words and hangs up.

"Well?"

Nick slides back in and swallows some of the by-now lukewarm brew. "She has to take her kid to her sister's. Then she'll pick us up here."

"She has a *kid?*"

Nick shrugs. "Why not?"

"Are you sure she is what we think she is?"

"Keep your voice down, will you? Sure I'm sure. Why else would she agree to meet two total strangers in a diner?"

Some idiot has put another nickel in the jukebox and it swings into "My Heart Has A Mind Of Its Own" for the third straight time.

"You know what I think we should do? I think we should get on the next bus and hightail it out of here."

"Jesus, Ryan, don't be so jumpy. She sounded very cool, like it's no big deal to her, like she does it every day of the week."

"Cripes."

"It's all going to be fine, I tell you."

"This is the middle of nowhere," I complain. "How are we going to get back to school by six?"

"We won't turn into pumpkins if we're not back by six. My aunt had a flat tire."

"Oh, I see."

"On a back road," Nick says, pulling on his big nose. "Miles from civilization."

"What were we doing on a back road? I thought we were having tea at the Eatonville Inn."

"My aunt was looking for her great-grandmother's grave, and we got lost."

"Her great-grandmother's bones are in Italy."

"No, this aunt is on my mother's side of the family," Nick replies. "We found a jack in her car, but it turned out she'd saved it from her previous car, which was a VW, and this was a Plymouth, and it didn't fit. So then you and I walked five miles to a farmhouse, but they didn't have a phone. They did, however, have a jack they thought might fit the Plymouth, but unfortunately it was in the bed of the pickup their son had just left in to go fetch a load of cow manure and—"

"Cow manure in February?"

"Okay, firewood and—"

"Old Cornball is not going to believe one word of this. He's going to phone your father who will inform him you don't have an aunt and—"

"I do so have an aunt."

"Where is she?"

"Seattle, last I heard."

"And then, Old Cornball is going to put us on detention for the rest of our natural lives."

"Come on," Nick says, sliding out of the booth. "We're supposed to wait for her under the sign outside."

We position ourselves, as instructed, under the neon sign that says CROW DIN R BU GERS F T FOR A K NG. A yellow crown on the sign blinks on and off. A couple of cars pull into the parking lot, but one has a guy in it and the other disgorges two overweight women. A little light snow begins to fall.

"Maybe she came and went while you were combing the country-side for a jack."

"Nah," Nick says, ignoring my feeble attempt at humor. "She said she'd be a while, and we should keep our socks on."

"Maybe her kid got sick at the last minute. Or her car wouldn't start."

"Stop worrying. She'll be here."

The Eatonville bus swerves off the service road, crunches over an empty beer can, and halts in front of the diner. As the engine idles and wipers thrash, three passengers—a woman accompanied by two kids in snowsuits—get off and a man wearing a sheepskin coat climbs aboard. The guy walks casually to the back of the bus and takes off his coat and stuffs it into the overhead compartment. "That's the last bus to Eatonville for an hour and a half," I remark.

"Should be just about the right amount of time."

The folding glass doors wheeze shut and the bus eases forward. Brake lights flashing, it hesitates a moment before pulling onto the service road. I keep my eyes on it until it reaches the highway, passes a semi, and disappears around a bend.

At the pumps a guy unscrews the cap to the gas tank of his pickup and pokes the nozzle in. His girlfriend, or maybe his wife, waits in the cab, listening to a country-western tune on the radio. She turns the rearview mirror toward her and begins to apply lipstick, sucking her lips inward to spread it from the upper lip to the lower. The guy saunters over to the diner to pay for the gas, and at the same time the woman with the kids in snowsuits come out, unwrapping candy bars. They get into a van and drive away, the torn wrappers skittering across the parking lot.

By now Nick's dark hair and the shoulders of his leather jacket have collected a dusting of snow. I search my pockets for a tissue to staunch my runny nose and come up with one linty cough drop and a paper clip. I feel myself beginning to shiver, and I'm also a little lightheaded. Coming down with the flu, probably. I envision myself losing consciousness and crashing onto the tarmac, splitting my head open and requiring seventeen stitches. Morosely I wonder how Nick will weave that detail into our story for Old Cornball.

A car—gray, nondescript, of uncertain vintage—pulls up beside us, and a woman who's maybe in her early thirties winds down the window. "Need a lift?" she asks. She has a lit cigarette in her hand.

"We're waiting for somebody," Nick says.

"I'm the somebody," she replies. "Get in."

Nick walks around to the passenger side and I get in the back. When the woman has started off I notice a doll on the seat beside me.

A naked doll, with tightly braided Dynel hair and a bellybutton. Something about that bellybutton gets me. I turn the doll over onto its face.

"Sorry to keep you boys waiting," she says, and the transmission gives a sudden lurch as she picks up speed on the service road.

"That's okay," I say.

"You know how it is."

"Sure," Nick says.

I have to do something about my dripping nose. On the seat near the doll I find a crumpled paper napkin. Surreptitiously I wipe my nose with it and then, unable to figure out how else to dispose of it, roll the napkin into a ball and tuck it in the crack between the seat and the seatback.

The woman cracks open her window and tosses the butt out. She takes the next exit off the highway and turns right at the end of the ramp. We pass an auto supply store and a couple of gas stations and some vacant storefronts, cross a sullen ice-choked little river, and now we're in a more residential area. Small prefab houses with metal awnings, scrubby yards separated one from the other by hedges of pricklebush, dim porch lights, no sidewalks. The snow has stopped falling. Dusk will soon be upon us.

"Where you boys from?" the woman asks.

"New York," Nick tells her.

"New York?" She turns left and the doll slides slightly closer to me. "What brings you to Meecham?"

We've already agreed on the undesirability of revealing our St. Bart's connection, or in fact anything else specific about us, so Nick says, "Just passing through."

"Passing through." She laughs. "I wouldn't mind doing that myself."

She pulls into a driveway and shuts off the engine. I'm not sure what I expected (sleazy motel with metal lawn chairs rusting in the elements? Downtown hotel with burned-out light bulbs in the dank corridors?) but this certainly isn't it. A square one-story house, white, with a tricycle on the porch and a Christmas wreath hanging from a nail on the door. Dry needles sprinkle onto the mat as she unlocks the door and pushes it open.

Though small, the house doesn't seem to have enough furniture: in the living room a couch and beanbag chair only, and in the dining ell a card table with two folding chairs. The carpet (tan with narrow brown stripes, dirty) is littered with Lego blocks and puzzle pieces and broken plastic toys. There's an aroma of stale cigarette smoke, sour milk, and piss. Cats, maybe. Or soaking diapers. Or the kid maybe has accidents on the carpet.

She takes off her car coat and flings it into the beanbag chair. She's slim, narrow-waisted, wearing those pants that are cut off in mid-calf and a flimsy T-shirt that reveals the outlines of her bra. Pretty, the way a girl standing ahead of you in line at the Dairy Queen might catch your attention for the time it takes to reach the guy squeezing soft ice cream into paper cups. You'd never think of her again, though.

"You fellas are kind of young," she says. When she speaks, I can see that one lower tooth crosses over the one next to it. I find that attractive, more so than the teased dirty-blond hair or cone-shaped breasts under the T-shirt.

"Eighteen," Nick tells her.

"Yah, right." She looks us over a moment more and then says, "What kind of recompense are we talking about?"

Nick's eyes bug at the incongruity of the word "recompense." "Uh, my friend mentioned thirty-five." For the first time I detect a hint of nervousness in Nick.

"Thirty-five *each*, you understand."

"Of course," Nick says.

"You can give it to me now."

I take my wallet out of my jeans pocket and extract a folded wad, secured with a rubber band, that contains five fives and ten ones. Money I earned last summer cutting lawns around town and was saving to buy a stereo. "I guess you don't take American Express," Nick says, but she doesn't crack a smile. He hands her his money, and she counts it, and mine too, and thrusts the bills into the pocket of her clamdiggers. "Okay," she says briskly. "Who's first?"

"Be my guest," I say to Nick.

She disappears into the shadows of a short hall off the living room, Nick behind her. I sit on the couch and pick up a rumpled *Family Circle* off the carpet. Leafing through it, I find instructions for making tree ornaments out of a sort of dough that when you bake it becomes hard like plaster. Then you paint it and apply glitter. One is a candy cane ornament made out of two coiled snakes of dough.

As if through cotton batting I hear water running, some mumbled conversation, the single squeal of a bedspring.

I focus hard on the illustration of a Santa ornament, and what it makes me remember is coming into the house in my wet snowsuit after sledding. I smell ginger cookies baking. My mother's taking a pan of them out of the oven. As quiet as I can I sneak up on her, but when she turns to look at me, the baking pan in her hands, I can't get her face right. It's as if I'm seeing her through water, or my eyes are bleary, the lashes stuck together with mucus. The only face I can conjure out of memory is the skeletal face of her last weeks.

In no time at all Nick appears in the doorway. His shirt is half-buttoned, his belt ends dangling from the loops on his jeans. "Your turn," he says.

I know I can't do this, not here, not with her. "Let's go, Nick."

"What do you mean? You already paid. I bet she won't give it back."

"I just want to get out of here."

Nick's right, she won't return my money. She needs it to pay the rent, she says. She does, however, drive us to the Crown Diner on her way to pick up her kid, and we're in plenty of time for the bus. We make it back to school far later than the time we signed out for, but by some miracle Old Cornball never says a word about it. Nick and I do not speak of the trip to Meecham to anyone, not even each other.

3. 1967

In with Nick come the smells of mothballs and wet wool, tracks of muddy slush, and luggage consisting of a moldy-looking army surplus backpack. "Why didn't you let me know you were coming? How'd you get here?"

"Greyhound."

This house was once a lumber baron's mansion, and my apartment is half its ground floor. Now the building has fallen on hard times, but it still boasts such amenities as fifteen-foot ceilings and indoor shutters. The landlord would not be pleased to see slush melting on his hardwood floor.

"So how was Paris?"

"It had its ups and downs. Not a great place to be if you're broke, actually."

Nick slings the backpack off his shoulder and strips himself of the oversized mothbally coat, which looks like something Raskolnikov might have worn for hiding out in a damp cellar. In the past few years Nick's taste has run to coats found in bus terminals, shoes and shirts purchased from thrift stores, self-administered haircuts. These economies are how he buys his freedom, he likes to claim, though I've noticed he's not above sponging off people when it suits him.

"Where'd you find that relic? Left Bank flea market?"

"The coat? West Hartford. Out in front of my apartment, lying on top of a heap of trash."

"West Hartford, Connecticut? You have an apartment there?"

"I'm back in school," Nick announces gloomily, "as of three weeks ago. University of Hartford this time. Got any beer?"

Out in the kitchen I open the refrigerator and seize a couple of bottles of Schlitz. It's been going on a year since I've laid eyes on Nick. But it seems longer. In the meantime I've been recovering from a failed romance, among other depressing activities, and Nick's been in Paris doing God-knows-what.

"How come you decided to go back to school?" I ask on my return from the kitchen.

Nick sits on the sofa with his bottle of Schlitz and pries off the cap, using a small multipurpose tool on his keychain. I remember when Nick acquired this, a souvenir lifted from a girl during a wild spring-break party in Boston freshman year. The cap bounces off the coffee table and skids under the radiator.

"My old man exerted a certain amount of pressure." He takes a drink. "And then there's the draft board."

"Double whammy."

"From now on, I'm toeing the line. Sticking to the straight and narrow."

"Glad to hear it," I say, wondering how long this resolution will last.

Nick sets his beer bottle on the table and begins to fiddle with the keychain gadget. He opens it so all the tools are spread around in a pinwheel: tiny scissors, nail file, corkscrew, knife blade, tiny screwdriver. "If you don't mind me saying so, Ry, you don't look so great. What's going on?"

I'm really glad to see Nick. He has a way of turning up when I'm low, as if he had an eerie sixth sense about me. "Oh . . . one thing and another."

"Such as?"

I empty most of my beer in a few gulps and then rummage the room for cigarettes. In view of the numbers of souls currently being maimed or annihilated in Vietnam, not to mention numerous other social disruptions, my father's engagement to a flighty ignoramus seems too trivial to mention. "Ah, just the usual junk. Papers due, some flu bug eating me."

"Hm." Nick swishes some beer around in his mouth like mouthwash and swallows it. "You don't seem very settled," he remarks.

"Settled?"

His dark eyes move from the chandelier, cobwebs strung across its fake brass arms, to dusty boxes of unpacked books. "Moved in."

He's right about that. Since taking this apartment in September I've been more or less camping out here. That was the same month Marybeth called and broke the news about our father's upcoming foray into matrimony, and I have to confess I'm still stewing over it.

Finally I locate a pack of cigarettes under a textbook, light one, and walk to the window. It's snowing a bit, leaving a gritty layer on top of filthy snow banks that have been around since November and will probably last until June. In my palm my mother's old Ronson feels smooth from much handling and oily with lighter fluid. "My dad's getting married," I suddenly tell him. "Can you believe that?"

"No kidding. Is that what's got you down?"

It takes me a while to answer. "Maybe."

"Who is she?" Nick asks from the sofa.

"Oh, some birdbrain gold digger he met at church," I say irritably.

"This may come as a surprise to you, but your old man doesn't have any gold."

"I just can't figure out why he'd do it."

"Maybe he loves her."

"Huh."

"It happens, even to old guys like your father. Anyway, you're a big boy now. It's not like your stepmother's going to be yelling at you to comb your hair and brush your teeth."

Even the word stepmother annoys the hell out of me. Grunting, I poke the half-smoked cigarette into the heap of filters in the ashtray.

"What you need," Nick goes on, "is a break. A change of scenery."

I know what he has in mind. We've gone off on these middle-of-the-term excursions before. The Boston fling. Another time we stayed in Nick's house when his parents were on a vacation in Italy, a revel that ended in a modified orgy with a couple of Mt. Aloysius Junior College girls on the living room floor. Then there was the cheap winter rental in Marshfield—those girls we picked up from a local grocery along with bags of Fritos. Nick seems to draw energy from these episodes. Unfortunately, the opposite is true for me. "I thought you're toeing the line from now on," I say.

"There's toeing and toeing."

I return to the kitchen for another beer and Nick follows, shuffling in too-big wing tips. "Got anything to eat?" Nick asks.

From the cupboard over the sink I glean a box of soda crackers that were there when I moved in and a nearly empty jar of peanut butter. From the refrigerator, jars of pickled herring and green olives and two more bottles of Schlitz.

"Is that all?"

"What did you expect, a banquet?"

"A feed like this is enough to give a person nightmares," Nick mutters, peering into the peanut butter jar.

"Now that you mention it . . ."

Suddenly Nick is alert. Sophomore year at St. Bart's, Nick became fascinated by Jungian dream theory. Every morning during the walk between chapel and first period he'd excavate my unconscious mind for material to interpret according to Jung. Half the time I had to invent dreams portentous enough to make Nick happy. Now he insists that I give him examples of my recent dreams, and I start to tell him about one that took place in a post office.

"A post office?" he asks skeptically.

Evidently he doubts the possibility of a meaningful drama transpiring in a post office, or anyway, the kind of bland prefab P.O. we have back home in Jersey. "This wasn't just any post office," I assure him. "It was huge. Cavernous. I was at the end of an interminable line, holding one of those slips that tell you they tried to deliver a parcel but you weren't home. It was very important that I get this parcel—"

"Why?" Nick is scraping the bottom of the peanut butter jar with a fork.

"Cut that out, will you? The sound gives me the willies."

"What's important about this particular parcel?"

"I don't know. That was just part of the dream. I had to get it, but I was also late for some other appointment—an exam I had to take, I think—and the line was barely moving at all."

Nick licks peanut butter off the tines of the fork. "And?"

"Well, when finally I get to the front of the line I see the package in some kind of cubby hole behind the counter. I don't know how I know it's mine, but I do. Then I discover I don't have the yellow slip. Somehow I've lost it. Naturally the clerk—he's a pudgy, balding guy, a real old fart—refuses to give me the parcel. He says I have to show him I.D. And then I realize I don't have my wallet, either. I can't prove I'm me! I'm pounding on the counter in such absolute frustration, I feel like strangling the guy. Goddammit, I *am* going to strangle the guy. I reach across the counter, stretching so the edge of it is cutting into my gut, but he's backing up and I can't . . . quite . . . reach . . . his . . . neck."

Nick drops the fork on the table and leans his back against it, rattling several crusted saucepans. "So once again your father manages to escape."

"My father?"

"Is that the end of the dream?"

"No, there's more. Suddenly, to my surprise, the clerk gives up and hands the package over."

"How big is this package?"

"Oh, maybe the size of a small shoebox. A little kid's sneakers would fit in it nicely."

"Go on."

"Everybody in line gathers around and watches me tear off the brown wrapping paper. Somehow a hunting knife has materialized in my hand—"

"—a hunting knife?"

"—and now I'm slitting open the tape on the box. Inside the box is…"

I've got Nick's complete attention. "Is what?"

"That's when I wake up."

"Figures," Nick says.

We carry our beers back to the living room. After he's settled again on the landlord's ratty sofa, Nick asks, "This box have any heft to it?"

I try to place myself back in the dream. "A fair heft," I decide, "considering it's not very big."

"Like it could have pebbles in it?"

"Maybe."

"Ashes, maybe? Bits of bone?"

I look at Nick. Suddenly I remember something I haven't thought of in years, possibly since it happened. I'm sitting on the front stoop with Marybeth. Early spring, no leaves on the trees yet. It's chilly, drizzling, and she's crying. Tiny droplets of rain collect on the sleeve of her cardigan. This must be, I realize, just after Mom died. A big car drives into the driveway and a man in a black suit gets out with a box in his hand. Marybeth and I shove over on the stoop and he steps up past us, rings the bell, and hands the box to my father. "Thanks for bringing it over," my father says. "Appreciate it." Wasting no time in chit-chat, the man gets back in the car and drives away. When Marybeth asks my father what's in the box, he won't tell her, and we never see it again. Now I know.

"That's it," I say to Nick. "Ashes and bits of bone."

"You gotta bury it, Ryan."

"How can I, when I don't have it?"

"You really want to know?"

I think this over for a minute. "Yeah. I do."

"Give your old man your blessing. Ten years is long enough to grieve. Too long."

I don't want to admit it, but I know he's right.

This visit Nick doesn't stay long. Monday morning I'm back in class and he's on the Greyhound headed down to West Hartford, toeing the line. I decide to quit smoking. I keep the Ronson around where I can see it, but never use it again.

REAPING TARES

Alison envied Zoë MacQuarrie everything about her apartment: the fireplace of milky gray marble; the size of the living room, luxuriously spacious for one person; the tall windows curtained in gauze. Sipping Dry Sack, Alison and Rob sat on a couch upholstered in olive-green velvet, while Zoë perched opposite them in the single armchair. A basket held dry pods on long stalks, ugly but striking. No rugs distracted from the varnished floorboards; no pictures cluttered the walls. It occurred to Alison that what she liked most about the place was its emptiness, its air of as-yet-unfulfilled possibility. At a discreet volume, string players made music on CD.

"However did you find this place?" Alison asked. "I thought apartments in these buildings are passed down from generation to generation. You know, like heirloom brooches."

Zoë explained that the former tenant, an old classmate, had taken it into her head to marry a dreary man and move to an equally dreary city in the Midwest. "She was stuck with the lease. I decided I'd do her a favor and take it over." Zoë dimpled, showing very white teeth. "The marriage won't work out, of course, but I never got around to telling her that."

Rob laughed appreciatively.

"Steal of a rent for Back Bay," Zoë confided. "So here's to divorce." She lifted her glass to Alison. "And to my brilliant lawyer."

Alison smiled, acknowledging though not really accepting Zoë's praise. A simple matter, the divorce proceedings: no children to negotiate over, little defense presented on behalf of the respondent. Compared to most of the cases Alison litigated, a snap.

"Honestly, I'm grateful," Zoë went on. "You made it all as comfortable as it could possibly have been, considering what a bastard Colin is."

Colin MacQuarrie was a black-humored New Zealander who'd made a bundle doing something with computers, a man just eccentric enough to provide melodramatic detail for a divorce complaint. In spite of her sympathy for Zoë as a victim of her husband's instability, however, Alison couldn't help feeling troubled by the ease with which she had skewered MacQuarrie and his attorney, a bumbler notorious in the profession for laziness and incompetence. Probably MacQuarrie picked Bubar the Boob out of a phone book: Just because you're smart about one thing, doesn't mean you're smart about everything. During the hearing in the judge's chambers Alison had been aware of MacQuarrie's sorrowful, inarticulate gloom; she sensed that he cared about his wife and grieved over losing her. No question Zoë was attractive, with her creamy skin and large hazel eyes, her infectious laugh. After the judge's ruling MacQuarrie returned to Auckland, leaving a considerable chunk of his life's earnings in Zoë's bank account. She would never have to go back to selling futons.

They dined by candlelight at a table placed near the windows. Lentil soup, followed by veal in a thick sauce served with baby carrots and pearl onions, followed by a sweet dark cake crammed with brandy-soaked figs. Although Alison had to be flattered by Zoë's prodigious efforts in the kitchen—most clients expressed their gratitude by sending a box of grapefruit, if that—the rich food lay in Alison's stomach like a clump of damp papier-mâché. With their second bottle of Lambrusco, Zoë described a trip she expected to take in the spring. "The Holy Land," she said. "Very highbrow, droves of biblical scholars and archaeologists along. Physically arduous, too, according to the brochure. Not a tour for little old ladies."

"You mean you'll be trudging around in the desert?" Alison asked. "Scaling Mount Ararat?"

"Mount Ararat's in Turkey," Rob said.

"We'll be climbing hills, if not mountains." Zoë tucked a bit of frosting into her mouth. "I'm going to have to get in shape for the trip, maybe hire a personal trainer."

After the cake Zoë poured coffee from a silver pot. "Cigarette?" she asked, and Rob took one, even though he'd quit. Or almost. If he never bought a pack, he claimed, but only smoked those offered him, sooner or later his nicotine craving would die of its own accord. Zoë leaned forward to light her cigarette from the flickering candle, then passed the candlestick to him.

Rob began to speculate on why God had led the Israelites out of Egypt on such a wildly circuitous route. A strategy to thwart dangerous enemies? An opportunity to turn the shackles of slavery into the shackles of faith? Rob smiled, taking a drag off his Tareyton. Or was it a sort of cosmic board game, perhaps? God's casual entertainment, employing Moses as a pawn that might reach the final square . . . or might not.

Zoë fixed her hazel eyes on his bony, intelligent face. "Depending," she said, "on the roll of the dice."

"Exactly. Here's this obstacle, the Red Sea. Can little Moses make it across? God shakes the dice. Luckily for Moses, it's a go, and Pharaoh's army drowns. God shakes the dice again. Uh-oh, bad news for the chosen people. Major detour through the desert."

"Past the Little Bitter Lake, to the Wilderness of Sin."

"Did you make that up?" Rob asked, impressed.

"My daddy's a preacher." Zoë laughed her throaty, smoky laugh. "Back in Sunday school," she said, "it occurred to me that when God informed the Israelites that they were His chosen people, maybe He was jiving them. Stringing them along so they'd toe the line."

"Pretty cynical, for a kid."

"Do you think so?" she asked innocently.

"Or," Rob said, "Moses could have improved on God's pronouncements when he relayed them to the Israelites. Embroidered them for his own purposes. We have only his word for what God said, right?"

Exhaling a cloud of smoke, Zoë said, "Moses never did get to the

Promised Land. There he is, within spitting distance, up on Mount Pisgah, looking across the Jordan River at the valley of Jericho. All this, he assumes, is about to be his. Then God pops out of a bush or something and says, 'I'm letting you eyeball it, boy, but no way are you going there.'"

"Do not pass Go. Do not collect two hundred dollars."

By now Alison felt as if she herself had been wandering in the wilderness for forty years, her stomach full not of manna but of veal in cream sauce and figgy cake. "I'm afraid," she said, "I have an appointment first thing tomorrow morning. Splendid dinner, Zoë."

"Let's do it again soon." Zoë slid the pack of Tareytons across the table to Rob. "Why don't you take one for the road?"

In the car Alison felt chilly and turned on the heater. September all right, no mistaking it, as if on the first of the month somebody had thrown a switch. "I wish you wouldn't bum cigarettes," she said. She knew he was enjoying planning when he'd smoke Zoë's Tareyton.

Their breath began to fog the windshield and Rob moved the heater knob over to defrost. "People don't mind."

"I mind."

"Interesting taste in music, I thought. Schubert. One might have expected seventies pop or Windham Hill." He maneuvered the Mazda onto Storrow Drive. "So what did the guy do?"

"Which guy are we talking about?"

"Zoë's husband. To make her decide to dump him."

"Privileged information, you know that."

"Come off it, Allie. The man's in New Zealand. I'm not going to run into him on the street." For a moment he laid his hand on the breast pocket of his herringbone jacket, as if to reassure himself that the cigarette was still tucked inside, then returned his hand to the wheel.

Alison hated the legalistic primness that crept into her voice sometimes; she couldn't blame Rob if he were to interpret it as petulance. Reluctantly she said, "He smashed a few windows."

Rob considered this. "With his fist."

"With a kayak paddle."

"Ah. Upscale type of brute."

Rob was happily piecing together a false image of the man, but what did it matter? Alison's upper back muscles tensed with cold. She huddled into her coat.

"What else did he do?" Rob asked.

"Nothing."

"Must have been *some*thing, if he's springing for Back Bay—steal of a rent or no—and the Holy Land."

"He pushed her piano out the door of their condo. It landed on a brick patio."

Rob chuckled, but asked no more questions.

Somewhat to Alison's surprise, Rob wanted to make love that night. He was more passionate than he'd been for a long time.

Rob was a slight man, fair hair beginning to gray, waist size nearly as small as Alison's. He worked as a freelance researcher and ghost writer for other people's books. Not the career he'd once envisioned, but he didn't apologize for it. Editors found him competent, fast, and reliable, and he made a reasonable living at the job.

He worked at home, a convenience allowing him to repair to the kitchen for coffee whenever he needed a pick-me-up, as well as exempting him from central-artery traffic or the T in rush hour. Alison relished the arrangement less than he. The nature of his job led him to amass prodigious quantities of manuscripts, books, old magazines, newspaper clippings, photos, and computer disks, which tended to creep out of his office when Alison was at work and take up residence in chaotic piles throughout the apartment. Moreover, even after a book he'd been party to was in print, he refused to dispose of any of the materials used to produce it, in case they might come in handy for some future project. If she moved one of the stacks to clear a surface, a crucial document would inevitably disappear.

The issue of Rob's packrat ways was a sore one, a source of dispute for most of the time they'd lived together. It was not, however, enough to break up a relationship over. Not like shoving a Yamaha spinet down two flights of steps.

In November, as a last-minute thought, they invited Zoë to Sunday brunch in their apartment: thirty or so friends and neighbors, writers that Rob knew through his work, a couple of attorneys from Alison's firm. Zoë, who arrived late, wore a high-necked Laura Ashley dress, too girlish for a woman in her thirties, which managed nevertheless to display the fullness of her breasts and complement her auburn-tinted hair. By contrast Alison felt scrawny in tailored black, her skin drained of color. Without glancing at the buffet table, Zoë went out to the balcony to smoke, and Rob promptly abandoned his laden plate to follow her. Hungry for a cigarette, obviously. Neither deigned to wear a coat, though the temperature was below freezing. Through the sliding glass door Alison could see their mingled smoke caught by the wind, and faintly hear their laughter.

Some weeks after the party Alison missed a period. Nothing new in that: Tension or fatigue often screwed up her cycle. This time, though, she seemed to need to urinate more than usual; a pimple erupted beside her nose; one morning in the elevator at Hallett & Bitterman she experienced a momentary dizzy spell.

Of course, it occurred to her that she might be pregnant, in spite of her precautions. What if she were? What then? She did not believe in marrying on account of a pregnancy; there could scarcely be a worse reason. Still, she and Rob had lived together for going on seven years. In two more she'd be forty. If she had to start out all over again to establish a relationship, she'd be past childbearing age by the time that transpired. If it ever did. She wasn't a beauty, had never possessed the knack of engaging the fascination of men. In any case, she didn't *want* to start over; the whole idea depressed her. She could not imagine living with a man other than Rob, adjusting to a whole new set of habits, revealing herself in intimate ways to some man as unfamiliar to her now as any anonymous rider on the T.

If she and Rob were going to marry, if they were going to have a child, now would be the time.

In truth, Alison's heart did not pulsate with envy whenever she saw a child in a stroller. Some women seem born to be mothers; she had no illusions that she was one of them. Nevertheless, she could not blithely turn her back on the possibility of motherhood, particularly if fate had landed it in her lap. Rather against her will, Alison had come to believe in—even count on—unlooked-for gifts, serendipity. The way she met Rob, for instance: Each without a companion, seated next to one another, they fell to talking during intermission at a performance of *A Doll's House.* What if Scott, in the office adjoining hers, hadn't been sent out of town on a probate case and offered her his ticket? Or if Rob's seat had been in row K instead of row J, or that night he'd come down with the flu? Not long ago she found a twenty-dollar bill on the sidewalk, just skittering along in the breeze, no owner in sight.

A week after the missed period Alison stopped off in a drugstore on the way to work and bought one of those do-it-yourself kits. She would run the test during her lunch hour, and then consider how to approach Rob with the news, if there was news, and decide what she herself wanted to do about it. But at quarter to twelve she received a phone call. "I'm downtown Christmas shopping," Zoë said, "starved and worn to a frazzle. Why don't you meet me for lunch?"

With her foot Alison shut the desk drawer in which she'd placed the cardboard box from Rite Aid, as if Zoë could see it over the phone. "I'm kind of tied up here. I have a case coming to trial next week."

"Oh, come on. Live a little."

Alison found it hard to say no to Zoë's teasing insistence without sounding dull as dishwater. They met in a restaurant around the corner from Alison's office building, a place that specialized in gourmet sandwiches. Zoë's cheerful face was flushed from the cold. She shrugged out of her coat and ordered a glass of Zinfandel with her ham and Boursin on Bavarian rye. Alison decided on seltzer with lime, and grilled chicken breast on whole wheat.

As they ate Zoë talked about Colin MacQuarrie's "whining" letters from Auckland; her decision to stay in Boston over Christmas, in spite of an invitation to visit friends on their gentleman's farm in upstate New York; a new CD featuring solo cello that Zoë had just purchased for herself. Other than the square, flat Tower Records bag on the corner of the table, Alison saw no evidence of shopping. There was a brief silence and then Zoë, fingering a crust from her sandwich, said, "What's the name of that mold—the one that grows on rye plants? It's poisonous, I seem to recall."

Where did this topic of conversation come from? Alison wondered.

"You could kill somebody that way," Zoë mused, "if you had somebody to kill."

"I don't, last I noticed."

But Zoë was getting into this now. "You could grind infected rye grain into flour and then bake it into bread. Or cakes, if you added enough flavoring."

"Hm," Alison said.

"Hey, I just had a terrific idea." She grinned, her teeth startlingly white, almost as if they weren't real. "Rob could use it in his book."

"His book." Rob's current project was converting an 800-page treatise on global economics into recognizable English. "What book?"

"That day I came to your place for brunch, he told me about the novel he's working on."

"You must have misunderstood." Alison had finished her grilled chicken, was thinking about the box from Rite Aid in her desk drawer. "What Rob writes are other people's books: autobiographies of politicians and popularizations of monographs and so on. Nobody poisons anybody, not literally."

Zoë, however, persisted. "He said it's a long novel full of Byzantine entanglements. The consequences of mysterious deaths reverberating through generations. How could I have misunderstood that?"

"Look, Zoë. If Rob were writing a novel, I'd know about it. That's not the sort of thing anyone—especially Rob—would be able to keep hidden for very long."

"Just run the idea by him, okay?" she said sweetly. "Tell him it's a present from me."

With deliberation Alison read her watch. "I've got to run, I'm afraid," she said, lifting her check from the table.

Back at Hallett & Bitterman, Alison ripped open the box, produced a urine sample in the john, locked her office door and waited the required ten minutes.

Negative.

Alison did not mention to Rob her lunch with Zoë, or the poison-rye plot device, or his supposed novel-in-progress. Fueled by several Bloody Marys, he must have invented this magnum opus to puff himself up, and gullible Zoë had bought it. Well, why shouldn't she? To most people, a writer is a writer, period. Alison didn't care to embarrass him by exposing his wishful thinking, which, befuddled by alcohol, he failed to foresee Zoë would reveal to Alison. Poor Rob.

As had become their custom, they planned to have a few people over for New Year's Eve—old friends, informal dress—and when Rob suggested inviting Zoë, Alison replied that probably she'd already have lined up a celebration more exciting than a quiet evening of literary and political chitchat. But at once Zoë accepted, telling Alison on the phone she now regretted having stayed in the city for the holidays. "It's not the same these days," she added, and Alison guessed what was happening: In the view of hostesses, a couple that includes a talented and exotic, if temperamental, New Zealander is one thing; a recent divorcée with no great accomplishments of her own, other than the ability to charm men, is another.

Zoë didn't have much to say that evening. Since Alison could not appear so cruel as to banish the smoker and her moocher to the sub-zero temperature on the balcony, the two of them periodically vanished into Rob's office. Smoke leaked out from under the door. Alison felt annoyed, and on edge, but held her tongue. What would it achieve to make a scene?

The following Saturday morning, emptying pockets before taking clothes to the cleaners, Alison found a scrap of paper—a credit card receipt—in Rob's tweed jacket pocket. She noticed that on the back of the receipt, in his precise jagged handwriting, he'd penned a memo to himself: "Sowing tares in enemy's wheat fields," with a biblical reference: Matt. 13:25. She left it on his dresser and went off to run errands.

For some reason the scrap of paper stayed in her mind as she drove from supermarket to co-op food store to post office to dry cleaner. Although Rob was hardly shy to display his erudition when the circumstances called for it, peppering manuscripts with biblical allusions was not his style. She recalled that he'd worn the brown tweed jacket on New Year's Eve. When handing it over the counter, she smelled dank smoke in the wool.

At home, she put away the groceries and marinated a boneless tenderloin of pork for their dinner. Rob was out, having lunch with an editor and a prospective client—odd on a Saturday, come to think of it. Alison realized there had been an unusual number of such lunches lately, and when she politely inquired about them, he'd say something like: "The concept's intriguing, but I can't make up my mind whether there's a market for it, whether it's worth investing my time," or, "I'm not sure I see where the idea's going. I guess I'll mull it over for a while." Uncharacteristically indecisive for Rob, Alison thought now.

She went into their bedroom and took another look at the crumpled receipt, then searched the bookshelves in Rob's office for a Bible. He did not, apparently, own one. In his unabridged dictionary she read that a tare, a biblical word, is "a noxious weed, probably the darnel." She riffled back through the pages and found that darnel is "any of several grasses of the genus Lolium." On a sudden hunch she moved forward to the "r"s as far as rye. No pertinent entry. But ryegrass, directly below: "Any of several European grasses of the genus Lolium."

Tare equals darnel equals rye.

Grains of rye bearing a poisonous fungus, deliberately sown in an enemy's wheat field.

Alison squirted dishwashing liquid into the pan she'd used to roast the pork and turned on the hot water. From the living room, at the far end of the hallway, a string quartet on CD sawed dissonantly.

She scoured the pan and rack, left them in the drainer to dry. While she was wiping the stove, Rob came to the kitchen and said, "Aren't you through out here yet?"

"Not quite."

With his glass of port he sat at the walnut table. Alison had found the table in a used furniture store soon after they started living together. She'd scraped off layers of paint and sanded and sanded, rubbed most of a quart of linseed oil into the pretty, old wood. A rickety piece, though, held together underneath with staples and metal reinforcements at the junctures of legs to tabletop.

"Have I ever told you that I used to play the fiddle?" Rob asked.

"Yes, you've spoken of it." In fact, she'd heard the tale often. How, in college, he'd played with a chamber orchestra, which in those glory days boasted a certain reputation. In his senior year the ensemble had even gone on a European tour: Manchester, The Hague, Stuttgart, Milan.

Rob kept his violin in his office. The instrument inside the case seemed to Alison as arcane and off limits to her comprehension as the workings of some complex electronic machine. Vaguely it worried her, this aspect of Rob's life she'd had no part in.

Alison wrung out the sponge. The music screeching down the hallway was beginning to grate on her nerves.

"I've been thinking of taking it up again."

"Really?"

"The thing is, I'd probably have to start from ground zero."

"It might be like riding a bicycle," Alison said. "The essentials are stored in your bones."

"Maybe so." Rob kept his fingernails longer than most men, and carefully clipped. An audience would notice his hands—also his lean, ascetic face. He sipped from the port glass. "There's nothing so satisfying as making your own music," he said to Alison.

In the past, he'd taken no pains to conceal his opinion that she had a tin ear. "I believe you," she replied.

Rob set his sticky glass on the table and licked his fingers. "By chance Zoë knows someone who might be willing to give me lessons, a woman who lives in her building. She's an émigrée from the Czech Republic."

"Perfect."

"Zoë's setting up an audition for me."

"Go for it," Alison said, endeavoring to sound sincere. She saw that resurrecting this skill would enrich Rob's life. Still, deep down she hoped that, like Rob's novel, the project would turn out to be a will-o'-the-wisp.

Alison's period returned in January. She could not shake the feeling, however, that her body was secretly nurturing something. One lunch hour, browsing at Barnes and Noble, she came upon an oversize best-selling paperback about pregnancy. If she had conceived in November, by now she'd be eight weeks along. From the book's photographs she imagined the fetus within her: skull traced with veins, delicately visible ribs, clenched toes. Perhaps her abdomen swelled slightly. She found herself tilting her spine to accommodate a subtle shift in her center of gravity.

To herself she scoffed: Have you gone mad? You know perfectly well you're not pregnant, even if Rite Aid hadn't told you so. Thirty-eight-year-old women don't get pregnant just like that, definitely not by accident. You've heard of false pregnancy in bitches? Nothing but hormones run amok. And what would you do with a baby if you had one? Plunk it down in a corner of your office like a potted plant?

No, the secret wasn't a child, but something else—indefinable, yet real—that she felt growing within the warm shelter of her body.

On a Saturday evening in February, Alison and Rob went to Back Bay for cocktails: Zoë's birthday party. The centerpiece of the occasion, her birthday gift to herself, was a new Onkyo surround-sound stereo with NHT Super Zero speakers. The guests, who stood about eating meatballs from toothpicks, seemed mostly to be expatriate New Zealanders or computer nerds, remnants from her marriage. Awkwardly they all eyed the room for places to sit down.

"When do you leave for the Holy Land?" somebody asked Zoë over the busy classical music emanating from the Super Zero speakers.

"What? Oh, the Holy Land's on the back burner." She laughed. "You know how things tend to come up."

Alison found herself talking to a fortyish woman who revealed, in a nervously braying voice, that she'd met Zoë at a support group for divorcées. In addition to that group, Janice confessed, she also attended Al-Anon, since her ex was an alcoholic. Not a mean drunk, a sly drunk. Respectable. Never raised a hand to her or missed a day at the office. Eventually Janice had found out that he kept a quart of vodka in a duffel bag in his closet, another in a file cabinet at work. "With that kind," she said, "it can take quite a while before you catch the drift."

"If you aren't married to him anymore, why do you still go to Al-Anon?"

Janice looked startled at the question. "Going to groups every night isn't much of a life," she told Alison, "but it's a life." Across the room, Rob was manipulating the stereo system's controls.

Feeling a headache coming on, Alison went to Zoë's bedroom to retrieve the bottle of ibuprofen in her purse. On a wicker nightstand lay a leatherbound New Testament. She sat on the edge of the bed, next to a heap of winter coats, and turned to Matthew 13:25. *While his men slept, his enemy came and sowed tares among the wheat, and went his way.* Then, in the next verses, Alison read the victim's solution for his enemy's treachery: To his men he said, *Let tares and wheat grow together until the harvest: and in the time of harvest I will say to the reapers, Gather ye together first the tares, and bind them in bundles to burn them: but gather the wheat into my barn.*

Behind her, particles of freezing rain begin to strike the window. She returned the New Testament to the night stand and extracted their coats from the pile on the bed.

In front of the fireplace Rob and Zoë stood close together in conversation, smoke curling over their heads. Alison gave Rob his topcoat, gently removed the cigarette from his hand, and tossed it onto the grate. "Sorry to rush off this way," she said to Zoë. "Sleet's coming down like crazy out there. The roads will be bad, and we have a long drive home."

At five A.M. Sunday morning Alison slipped out of bed and, on the computer in Rob's office, composed a letter. "Dear Mr. MacQuarrie," she wrote. "Although you don't know me, please be assured that I am writing as a friend.

"Possibly you are unaware that Barry Bubar, the attorney who represented you in the divorce action brought by your wife, has, on several occasions, been a defendant in legal malpractice suits. The plaintiffs were former clients who deemed themselves poorly represented by Mr. Bubar. This information can be verified by contacting the Massachusetts Bar Association.

"Your divorce is not yet final. I have reason to believe that if you were to request a rehearing of your case, with a capable attorney vigorously arguing your position, the outcome would likely redound to your benefit. At worst, your financial situation would almost certainly improve. At best, your wife might be inclined to re-examine her attitude regarding divorce."

In the fourth paragraph Alison listed the names and addresses of several respected divorce lawyers in firms other than Hallett & Bitterman. After printing the letter out on plain white paper, she stuffed it, unsigned, into one of Rob's el cheapo business-size envelopes and stowed it in her briefcase. She closed the document without saving and shut down the machine.

The next morning, once she'd located Colin MacQuarrie's address in a file in her office, affixed enough stamps to the envelope to dispatch it to the moon, and gone down in the elevator to mail it an outside box, she telephoned Zoë and invited her to lunch. "I have some exciting news," she planned to say over her glass of Chablis. "We're not telling people yet—that's why I didn't mention it at the party Saturday night. Of course, we're both thrilled."

In April, without ceremony, Zoë crated up her belongings and departed for Auckland. If, before she left, Zoë mentioned anything to

Rob about Alison's delicate condition, he's never referred to it. Nor has Alison questioned Rob concerning the novel-in-progress. Apparently lessons with the Czech émigrée didn't work out; the violin remains in Rob's office, nestled in its dusty, velvet-lined case. He has quit cadging cigarettes at parties. Perhaps his nicotine craving has, after all, given up the ghost, the way he always insisted it would.

Every now and then, when Alison and Rob are conversing in bed, the way people do after making love, the subject of marriage comes up. Without being difficult about it, Alison is resisting the idea. She has concluded that, on the whole, she likes things just the way they are.

THE LIFE OF THE MIND

We came down to the city from the Gotthard Pass, past stunted woods, chapels that needed mending, impoverished villages, and once in a while a ragged palm tree. It was August, 1964. This was not the Switzerland I'd imagined, not Heidi's, but for some reason I liked it better. Perhaps this down-at-heels country was more approachable than the perfect snowcapped version. Between drags on his cigarette Professor Zoppi related scraps of childhood memory. I concentrated on keeping the tinny little Fiat on the road.

The professor's gray hair was stiff as a porcupine's and his shoulders so narrow he could have bought his jackets in the boys' department. "The salient experience of my life," he said, tossing a butt into the dry weeds by the roadside, causing me to wonder how many conflagrations followed in our wake, "was to be a member of a minority within a minority. An Italian speaker in Switzerland. An intellectual in the Ticino." In fact, I knew, he'd spent much of his adult life outside his native land altogether, teaching in Australia, Canada, and finally Sacred Heart College in Chicago, where he and I had met. "Now, Cecilia, I'm in it again, up to my eyeballs," the professor said. *"Nella buona e nella cattiva sorte."*

I worked out the translation in my still book-bound Italian: For better or worse.

Bellinzona was hot and its inhabitants at lunch when we arrived, shutters closed over all the shop fronts. On the outskirts we eventually came to the villa, a square stucco structure on a street wide enough to be a boulevard, though utterly vacant at that hour. Over the mountains were spun out thin wispy clouds. The professor pointed out on the horizon three gap-toothed castles and their linked fortifications.

"Ominous," I said, only half joking.

"This has not always been a peaceful place."

A housekeeper had been hired long-distance, and she came to the curb with as many smiles and nods as a mechanical cuckoo announcing noon. Her hair was doused in henna, wattles jiggled at her neck. As she lugged our bags out of the backseat and across the walk, Frau Schissler spoke loudly in an all-but-unintelligible patois. Inside, the house smelled of long-ago meals, mold, antiquated plumbing; heavy curtains had been drawn across the windows to keep the place cool in the August heat. In the parlor, stacked up nearly to the ceiling, were cardboard boxes filled with books and other possessions, shipped ahead of the professor to await his arrival. The furniture was threadbare and mismatched, the patches of carpet visible between the boxes none too clean. A clock in a carved oak case ticked away in one corner, obviously having stood there marking time for generations of the professor's family, outliving nearly all of them. The professor had inherited the house from an ancient aunt and now expected to spend the rest of his days in the city of his birth.

Frau Schissler was explaining something to the professor with animated hand gestures. *"Mi dispiace,"* she said, shaking her head. "I regret, but . . ." Bit by bit I understood that she was not prepared actually to reside in the house; her grown son was ill— *"malatissimo"*—and needed her care. In spite of the professor's protestations about the agreement negotiated by his Cousin Ettore, spelled out in a document buried somewhere in the unpacked baggage, she remained adamant.

Now it struck me that there might be something a teensy bit unconventional—even risqué—about my coming here to be Professor Zoppi's assistant and the two of us living in this large empty house. It was one thing to have been his pupil and protégé at a Catholic college for women, where boyfriends never got above the ground floor of dormitories and even the remotest faculty office opened on a corridor thronged by chirping girls. Here there would be nobody but Frau Schissler, and she only in the daytime. Maybe my skittish parents had had a point, I thought, but I was less worried than curious.

As the housekeeper gabbled on to the professor, I wandered out to the back garden. Nothing much grew there except a sprawling olive tree, from which wash lines extended both to our house and to the windowless side of the next stucco building. Under the tree was a small table with a round metal top, its green paint chipping off.

Frau Schissler served our lunch there, or rather she left the food on the table and bicycled home to somewhere on the other side of the city. There were bottles of warm local beer, bread, a hard sausage, some grapes, and a block of cheese that reminded me of Fels Naptha.

We ate and drank mostly in silence. After a while Professor Zoppi gazed upward into the dusty leaves of the tree, where no olives hung. "It should have been pruned," he observed. "Olive trees must be pruned, or they are no good. Like poems." He lit a cigarette.

He'd never spoken of his connection to poetry before, either in his classes or to me privately. I was aware of it, of course; I'd gone to the library and looked up his biography when I was first drawn to him as a teacher and historian. Lazarro Zoppi had been a member of a small group of liberal Swiss intellectuals writing in Italian. In 1934 he won a locally prestigious prize for his poetry. But that same year he left Switzerland, became a professor of history and, so far as I knew, never published another poem.

"I'm glad I've come to Bellinzona," I said, my feeling of well-being stoked by beer and sausage. I ventured something inane about hoping his return to the home of his youth would stimulate a return to his first literary love.

"Oh, Bellinzona. Here they are deaf to poetry."

"Ah," I said, trying to hide my disappointment.

"Bellinzona is very good at clamor, celebration, *il carnevale, il dolce far niente.* Not so good at poetry. But perhaps that's just as well."
He put out his cigarette on his plate, amid scraps of sausage skin and

cheese rind, and with difficulty rose to his feet. I watched him limp to the house, arthritis hobbling his knees.

My father's parents emigrated from the Po Valley in 1901 and died when I was only a small girl; I have almost no memory of them. To me they are foreign-looking faces in photographs, their expressions as stiff as their Sunday-best clothes. My parents met and married in Cicero, the blue-collar suburb of Chicago where I was raised. Though of Italian background, both of them, they were determinedly *American* and never spoke more than a few words of their ancestral language, at least in my hearing. My father worked construction, and my mother was a cook in the cafeteria of the local parochial school, St. Margaret's. College for me, their only child, was something they acceded to, following the nuns' advice, but skeptical about what good it might do me. "Why don't she go to business school?" my father asked rhetorically after I'd already been accepted at Sacred Heart. "Learn a trade. What's wrong with that?" The truth is, I had little idea myself what college was supposed to be for. I did know, though, that I longed to have a remarkable life, and that I wasn't destined to stay in shabby Cicero, with its humiliating gangster reputation. The heck with typing and filing for a living.

In January of freshman year, as I was casting about for an elective to complete my schedule, my advisor talked me into taking Professor Zoppi's course in Italian cultural history. In my mind Italians were hapless peasants, uneducated like my grandparents, mired in poverty, stinking of garlic. But having no sensible alternative to suggest, I reluctantly agreed to sign up for the course

In spite of myself, I fell in love with it. Unlike the sisters at St. Margaret's, the professor had no interest in stuffing me full of countless dates and facts—although his casual familiarity with both impressed me. Without apparent effort he made coherent for me many centuries of events, taste, and invention. Gradually I came to understand that my own story as the grandchild of immigrants was a piece of something much bigger, forces seismic and inexorable, the aspirations and movements of whole peoples. And I discovered, with pride, how gloriously creative were my Italian forebears.

Professor Zoppi conveyed an overview of history, but he didn't neglect its particulars or its memorable characters. He relished the telling anecdote, the moment of comic surprise. Galileo is forced by the church to recant his claim that the earth circles the sun; but in his journal the physicist talks back: *"Eppure si muove!"* "Nonetheless, it moves!" Dante Alighieri parks Pope Boniface VIII, a real-life enemy, in the sixth ring of his *Inferno,* thus dooming the poor pontiff to eternal punishment. Caravaggio revolutionizes painting with his dramatically illuminated religious scenes—when he's not brawling in taverns or running from a murder charge. Garibaldi, the military unifier of Italy, writes President Lincoln offering to help subjugate the Confederacy—if given command of the entire Union army. "As you may be aware," the professor noted dryly, "he did not get the job."

I was enchanted by Professor Zoppi, even though the little man had a fussy, impatient side and was more than forty years older than I. Before I knew it I had become a history major and, to my parents' astonishment, taken up the study of the Italian language. Obsessed, I put such long hours into learning the elegant *lingua di Dante* that my mother fretted about my health—and my prospects. "Where are your friends?" she would ask when I was home from college. "Why don't you call them up, go bowling or something?"

"They're studying, Mom, like me."

"You know, Sissy, Mrs. Kasperzak from the church has a nephew, a nice boy . . ."

I informed my mother that I was definitely not interested in Mrs. Kasperzak's nephew, who probably had his beady eye on a law degree from NIU, after which he would make a bundle keeping sleazy clients out of jail. My attitude bewildered my mother. What's wrong with being a lawyer?

Of course Professor Zoppi was the advisor of my senior thesis, an exacting taskmaster. After several meetings in his office, he abandoned "Miss Piccolomo" and began to call me by my first name, pronouncing Cecilia in the Italian way, with a *chay* and a *chee.* I was ecstatic to have acquired such a romantic name. I resolved to leave behind my childish nickname forever.

When, upon my graduation and the professor's retirement from teaching in June of 1964, he invited me to accompany him to Bellinzona as his research assistant, I was so flattered that I never for a second considered any other course. An extended tutorial with the man who had already opened so much to me—and the chance to live in Europe, expenses paid—seemed all I could wish for. My mother and father, on the other hand, were aghast. All those sacrifices their parents had made to leave hardscrabble Europe behind, and now I demanded to go back there?

For his study the professor chose the large room at the top of the stairs that overlooked the front garden and had been the old aunt's bedroom. It had the best light, he said. The pink figured wallpaper was faded and the furniture massive. Two laborers hired by Frau Schissler moved an ink-stained desk up from a storeroom and a pair of glass-fronted bookcases from the parlor, dismantled the aunt's imposing *letto matrimoniale* and carried it and its horsehair mattress away. If the professor knew that the old lady had breathed her last in that bed—a detail Frau Schissler confided in me as she and I were unpacking boxes of books—it didn't apparently trouble him. On the wall he hung a framed woodcut of Dante Alighieri, whose hawk nose, disapproving scowl, and crown of laurel leaves lent an air of gravity to the room.

Professor Zoppi piled around him offprints of articles he had written on the Sonderbund and the Swiss Civil War of 1847, folders of photocopied documents, pamphlets, ragged pages of notes, stacks of books. His plan, he told me, was to stitch the articles together into a monograph, a project long delayed by the distractions of his teaching years. As he leafed through dog-eared pages and dictated notes, I took down what he said in improvised shorthand. Whether he was making progress or not was difficult for me to tell. I did know that Bellinzona housed no university or even a convincing library; the materials for the book would have to come out of the contents of this room and his own head.

Often the professor was sent a book to review by some scholarly publication. He would make his way slowly through it, cursing his eyesight, the stupidity of the author, and the shallow trickery of academic thought patterns. Then I'd type out his comments on his rattly portable Olivetti. After a few months I dared to omit some of the more ill-tempered passages.

One day when he was meditating out loud upon one of his articles, speculating how a point could be expanded upon, he paused for such a long time that I looked up from my yellow pad. How frail he seemed behind the big desk. *"Vedi,* Cecilia," he said. "I fear I have brought you here under false pretenses."

Nervously I wondered what he might mean.

"I must admit to you: I'm tired. My eyes . . ."

"You're probably coming down with a cold," I said.

And that's all it turned out to be. He took to his bed and stayed there for a week, wrapped in a frayed paisley dressing gown and drinking remedies prepared by Frau Schissler. Nevertheless, even when he'd recovered, progress on the book seemed dismayingly slow. No inspiration was involved, I perceived, just a dogged plugging along. The romantic in me wished he'd be more like the brilliant poet of his youth—or how I imagined that poet to have been. I wanted some of his genius to rub off on me or to touch my life in some way, if only second-hand. In any case, I needn't have been concerned about impropriety in my role. The professor treated me as would a grandfather: absentmindedly benign, occasionally crabby.

From the start Frau Schissler demurred from preparing dinner, though that's what she'd contracted by overseas mail to do. Many convoluted conversations centering on her son's nameless malady, which Professor Zoppi suspected to be either epilepsy or syphilis, and her responsibilities to him—greatly though she regretted any inconvenience this might cause the learned *signore*—resulted in our eating dinner every night in the neighborhood *trattoria.* I had to inspect the cutlery before use and discreetly pick clotted *ragù* sauce off supposedly clean plates. After two weeks of eating the same three entrées, rotated, I decided to be the cook. Soon that included marketing as well, since Frau Schissler's interpretations of my lists were approximate at best.

There were shops near the villa, but I preferred the greater selection—and the change of scene—in the town center. Canned and bottled goods I brought back in the Fiat. But two or three times a week I boarded the tram with my satchel and net bag to make the rounds of butchers and greengrocers, learning to elbow my way to the counters amid throngs of stout, black-dressed, jabbering housewives. At first I was disconcerted by the darkness of the non-grainfed beef and by how differently meat was cut, which led Professor Zoppi to make me a gift of his *Larousse Gastronomique.* Using its illustrations, I would find the cut I wanted in its French incarnation, translate the key word into Italian, and approach the butcher willing myself not to revert to "sirloin" or "sparerib." Choosing produce was child's play by comparison. Our diet, and my Swiss Italian, prospered.

By December there was no longer a variety of fresh vegetables in the market; I had to become more ingenious in my cooking. I wanted to. Not a simple matter to please the professor at table, but possible, and easier to achieve as a cook than as a wit. Coaxing a smile from him over my braised lamb shanks or *zuppa di fagioli* was satisfying. I began scouting the used bookstores for old cookery books, and that's how I met Gregorio.

Gregorio's shop was located in one of the narrow and cobbled streets of the oldest part of Bellinzona. A celebrated medieval watering trough stood only a block away, snarling up traffic at the center of an intersection. Gregorio had thinning fair hair, greenish eyes, and full brows that lowered and raised expressively when he spoke to me in his excellent though heavily accented English. His corduroy trousers were baggy and his cardigan out in one sleeve; he was the picture of a person who lived for the life of the mind, and I was attracted right away. With enthusiasm he searched his midden of books for additions to my collection, seeming to have all the time in the world to help me. In fact he had time aplenty, since few other customers stooped under the stone lintel to enter the murkiness of the shop. He appeared gratify-

ingly interested in me, and impressed by my exalted position as
Lazarro Zoppi's research assistant. I didn't tell him that there'd been
precious little research so far—on my part, at least.

It was only on my fourth drop-in at the bookstore that I learned,
to my chagrin, that Gregorio had a wife. One cold December afternoon he invited me upstairs to his flat above the shop for an espresso,
and there she was. Ceremoniously he sliced a piece of her birthday
cake for me, then dumped the cat onto the floor so I could have the
only chair that wasn't piled with books. He sat on the carpet, which
was studded with cigarette burns. Charlotte stood in front of a little
mirror teasing her brown hair to puff up in back.

Before her marriage Charlotte—spoken with three syllables—had
been an aspiring model. From Canton Sanct Gallen near the Austrian
border she'd gone to Milan to seek her fortune. What she'd found was
Gregorio, a fellow Swiss on holiday, and she eventually came back
with him to Bellinzona. They'd been married ten years; that winter
she celebrated her thirty-first birthday.

"When she finds a gray hair," he said to me in a stage whisper,
"she plucks it. One day"—he flicked five fingers in the air—"bald!"

"Not as soon as you," Charlotte replied in Swiss German-
accented English. She appeared to be examining her conjunctiva for
anemic tendencies. Her shoulders were broad for her frame, and she
was too short-legged to have been much of a model, I thought. Her
attractiveness had more to do with self-confidence than inherent
beauty. When she was moved to tell a story, taking the spotlight with
her laughter and fluttering hands, she was radiant. She aroused my
curiosity. Why had she not had children, for instance? How did she
fill her days, since she apparently didn't work in the shop? What had
she seen in Gregorio? She didn't seem the type to be attracted to
bohemian bookishness, but maybe ten years ago in Milan his cardigan
had not been out at the elbow.

Gregorio inquired about Professor Zoppi's plans.

"I think he's come home to stay," I said.

Reflectively he rubbed the thighs of his corduroys. "Cecilia must come and dine with us," he announced, without consulting Charlotte.

Meanwhile the professor's work on his monograph inched along. One afternoon a rickety gentleman in a fedora paid a visit, a fellow poet from the old days. Though his cane had a silver handle, his shabby coat was in serious need of a brushing. I hoped gossip and a glass of grappa would cheer the professor up, revive his enthusiasm for poetry, but I was disappointed. "In our youth we were idealists," he muttered afterward, when the friend had gone. "So certain that we, and only we, saw the light. *Cretini!*" Even in the December cold, Frau Schissler opened wide all the parlor windows to clear out the visiting poet's cigar fumes.

Gregorio's dinner party, when it happened, made up in conviviality what it lacked in culinary distinction. Grit in the risotto and gristle in the veal: *non importa.* Both Charlotte and Gregorio had what appeared to be an enormous capacity for wine, and he announced his intention to introduce me to as many varieties as possible. He opened a French vintage, then an Italian, then an Austrian.

"When it comes to wine," he declaimed in tipsy English, adding another bottle to a row of empties along the wall, "I am nonnationalistical."

"Nonpatriotical," Charlotte corrected, using her red fingernail to open a new pack of Gauloises.

At Gregorio's suggestion, on the last Saturday in January we drove into the mountains to visit a remote chapel he particularly admired. I'd borrowed the Fiat, since Gregorio did not own a car. Happily, Charlotte had declined to come along.

Our destination lay in deep woods, out of sight of other buildings. Our footsteps were the first to break the snow before the heavy wooden door. The Romanesque interior was narrow and unlit, with wooden chairs for no more than thirty worshippers. A simple altar framed a dark, bold painting of the crucifixion that was surely from the Baroque period, and I thought of asking about this. But I didn't like to break the silence, or intrude on Gregorio's evident communion with the tiny church. We stood side by side looking up at the much replastered ceiling, our breaths rising in visible puffs. After a time the shoulder of Gregorio's coat touched mine. "Cecilia," he said huskily, examining the vaulting above, "there is something I must confess to you."

A warmth of anticipation started in me, which was quickly diluted by guilt.

Gregorio turned to face me, his thin lips parted. "I am myself a poet," he whispered. Since the age of sixteen, he continued, he had been a passionate admirer of Lazarro Zoppi, not the academic whose career had ended at an obscure women's college in a Midwestern American city, I was to understand, but the liberal and nationalistic poet of the thirties, the member of the Instituto Editoriale Ticinese. Lazarro Zoppi's poems and his own were spiritually linked, Gregorio felt. He had written the *maestro* several times since learning, through me, of his return.

"I have informed him that I was born in Bellinzona and am alone in the Ticino in carrying on his aesthetic philosophy. But," he said sadly, "he does not reply."

Oh dear, I thought, knowing the professor's scorn for his own youthful idealism. Yet it seemed wrong to say that to Gregorio. Who was I to explain one Swiss to another? Besides, if the spark of the younger man's admiration were to rekindle the other's creative impulses—one couldn't rule out that possibility—it might give new purpose to the professor's life, as well as make it more interesting. I envisioned the parlor turning into a salon, with me as its gracious mistress, sort of like Alice B. Toklas, whose cookbook I'd just been reading. We'll all be better off, I thought, if he becomes a poet again. "Professor Zoppi's eyesight," I said at last, "has been failing in recent years."

"Yes," Gregorio exclaimed, "that must be it." His face lit up with renewed hope, and in the ensuing expectant pause I found myself inviting him and his wife to dinner at the villa. Not consulting the professor beforehand was a little daring. But he should know who my friends are, I reasoned. He will see the compliment in my presenting them to him. Gregorio accepted the invitation with alacrity, and when he told Charlotte, even she was pleased.

I cooked a beef and onion stew in beer and set the table in the dining room, a room the professor and I did not ordinarily use, because it was too large for the two of us. Around the table were chairs with upholstered seat covers the color of strong tea, and against one wall loomed a buffet with mirrors set at various angles to reflect and multiply the plates of food. Surprisingly, the professor had not grumbled when I broached the subject of the dinner party, and he gave me the money to buy two bottles of wine.

We dined late. Charlotte wore brown velvet, a dress that looked as though it had come down from some previous generation. She wore it artlessly, however, as if she hadn't guessed what the furnishings of the villa would be like and how perfectly she in that dress would fit into the surroundings. Her arms were bare. She talked to the professor about a sculpture garden she had visited near Copenhagen—she'd been photographed there wearing beaver and lynx. This must have been more than ten years before, I reckoned; she'd done no modeling since her marriage, yet in her conversation it seemed to have been the previous week. Her eyes were lively, and she spoke expressively in her accented English. We all spoke English that evening, not so much as a gesture to me, I suspect, but to enable the others to show they could.

By the time Gregorio succeeded in maneuvering the conversation around to poetry in general, and his own poetry in particular, we had emptied both bottles of wine and the professor was pouring out glasses of Benedictine. I feared the evening would end precipitously, the professor divining that he was being used, but instead he listened with patience and apparent interest to Gregorio's story: the laboriously written poems about the frustrations of life in the Ticino (its vulgarity, its lassitude, its cultural heritage that, although long, was without high points); the rejections from publications both great and small. "I don't mind so much being rejected, that is not the issue. To be *ignored,* that is what is hard."

"It is hard," the professor agreed, leaning over to light Charlotte's cigarette.

"Perhaps you might do me the great honor of looking at some of my poems—only a few, I would not waste your time."

"Certo. Sarebbe il mio grande piacere," the professor said, with only a whiff of irony, which I was sure Gregorio did not catch. Soon after that, pleading the weariness of an old man, the professor went to bed, and Gregorio, Charlotte, and I sat at the table for another hour. Gregorio, elated and expansive, was envisioning a sudden outpouring of artistic creativity in Bellinzona, sparked by the old professor, but actually drawing its energy from himself, the heir apparent. I couldn't help feeling excited myself.

Frau Schissler, I found, had not the authority to put a damper on this new social connection, however much she might complain. The next morning Gregorio bicycled to the villa with a large manila folder under his arm, and the professor, opening the study window and shouting down to Gregorio, who stood like Romeo in the sodden, wintry front garden, invited him and Charlotte to dinner the following Saturday.

That day I cooked chickens stewed with prunes, and Gregorio, investing in his future, brought two bottles of sweet San Merino sparkling wine.

Charlotte again wore brown: a different dress, made of some soft fluid material, cut low over her breasts and with short puffed sleeves. Her scent reminded me of nutmeg. It was remarkable, I thought, how she could leave her squalid flat behind her and be not at all touched by it. No snags in her nylons, no cat hair on her dress or butter stains on her glove. Gregorio was not similarly impeccable, but then, no one would have expected that of a poet.

This time Charlotte talked about Morocco—she'd been there, too, on a day trip from Spain. Somebody, an Arab, had given her a ring made of silver that had a hidden compartment you were supposed to fill with poison. What kind of poison she'd never found out, though, or what you were supposed to do with it. Perhaps, she hinted, it was to do yourself in if you were caught in a compromising situation. She spoke in rapid slangy Italian, and I didn't catch all of what she said. The professor laughed, and Gregorio looked uncomfortable.

Partly, I knew, he was cross because the professor had said nothing yet about his poems. He tried to change the subject to something more literary, but then the professor began to talk about Egypt, where he'd been as a young man. In 1923 or '24, he couldn't remember the exact year, he'd been secretary to a rich old man from Geneva who dabbled in travel writing as a hobby and who set off to report the opening of King Tut's tomb. Too late, though; the Tut market had already been glutted. "I was shat upon by camels from Alexandria to Luxor," Professor Zoppi said, smiling in a conspiratorial way at Charlotte.

"Oh yes, camels," she said, and giggled.

Gregorio gave me a strained look. I served the salad, not wanting to get involved in whatever was going on. However, I didn't like this turn of events any better than Gregorio did. I felt left out and ignored in my own dining room, by my own professor.

In the end he did get around to Gregorio's poems. "Very nice, I thought. Yes."

"Do you have some specific criticism, something I could use to improve . . ."

Professor Zoppi examined the back of his hand, as though noticing for the first time a liver spot there. "Well, that long poem about frescoes . . ."

"Yes," Gregorio said eagerly. "I call it 'La Volgarità.'"

"I thought the imagery was . . . not overstated, I will not say that . . . slightly lacking in precision, perhaps."

"Oh?"

"You might consider returning to have another look at that church." The professor, his bristly hair standing on end, folded his napkin and left us, bowing formally to Charlotte and to Gregorio.

Gregorio, chastened but full of energy, did go back to the church and reexamine the frescoes—twice. He arrived at the villa the next week with the rewritten manuscript. My Italian wasn't good enough to make fine distinctions, but the new version, when I read it, did seem less didactic and more descriptive.

The rainy season turned into spring. Charlotte presented me with a hibiscus in a clay pot, and the buds opened swiftly: one day—bang—an oversized and overdressed blossom, the next day a long shriveled tube.

Gregorio went careening about rewriting his poems. They got longer and longer, until I mentioned to him what the professor had said about the pruning of the olive tree. Then they got shorter and shorter. Whether expanding or cutting, Gregorio made the case to me that he was coming ever closer to Professor Zoppi's standard of excellence. As a consequence, he expected soon to benefit from the professor's influence in the literary world. Finally editors and house readers, those mean and capricious few, would be wrestled to the floor, metaphorically speaking.

"Influence?" I recall the professor saying to Gregorio over coffee in the parlor. The bookseller had taken to stopping by the villa with small gifts: a few ounces of chocolate with almonds or a yellowed chapbook by some prewar poet that had come across his path. "I have no influence," the old man said. Gregorio refused to believe him, convinced the professor was only being modest in his genteel, old-school way. The next day Gregorio and I stood in the back of the bookstore and he, gazing in bemusement at a beverage ring someone had left on the cover of a paperback copy of *Les Jeunes Filles en Fleurs,* said to me, "If only I could find the trick. *Il trucco,* you know, Cecilia? I'm sure that's all it is, because I'm so close."

Of course he was talking about his poems; that's all he thought about anymore.

"It's like the tiny section of false molding you press to open the secret door. When I have figured out what he wants from me, everything will fall into place." He smiled dreamily, no doubt imagining a judge draping a beribboned medal around his neck.

But I wondered whether the poems retained even the slightest vestige of meaning, jiggered with so. "Professor Zoppi once told me he didn't understand how poems should be written when he was young and writing them."

"He was published. He won a prize."

"Yes, but he renounces all that now."

"No, Cecilia." Gregorio looked at me with amused condescension. "He's come back to Bellinzona, don't you see?"

I was half convinced. He *had* come back.

As the weather grew warmer, Gregorio's desperation increased. Time was going by so rapidly; he was over thirty, already too old to be considered a young genius. If something didn't break soon, he'd have to settle for being a middle-aged genius.

One day when I was in town he invited me to have coffee with him, but rather than taking me upstairs to the flat, he shepherded me to a café around the corner and we sat outside under the awning. He lifted an ashtray full of someone else's butts and olive pits and dumped it out on the sidewalk. Without consulting me he ordered Cinzano instead of coffee. As always, he began to talk about Professor Zoppi, and I only half listened until he came to what was obviously the point of this meeting.

"Cecilia, I have concluded that before I am in a position to understand the professor completely, there is something I need to know and which only you can tell me." He took a deep breath and shifted his body so that our glasses rang on the metal table.

"Yes?"

"I am embarrassed," he said, frankly and pointedly, as though his embarrassment was the result of something I'd done.

"I'm sorry," I said, confused.

"What—exactly—is your relationship to Professor Zoppi?"

"I'm his secretary . . . and his cook."

"Nothing more?"

Finally I saw what he was driving at. "No, nothing more."

"No, of course." He looked relieved, but also puzzled. "I hope I have not insulted you."

"Gregorio, I think you are carrying this thing too far."

He sighed.

Things began to change then, in a way that made me uneasy. Charlotte came to dinner in a pink knitted dress the same color as the hibiscus; her nipples were erect and obvious under it. Gregorio, rather than looking impatient or resentful of his wife's long conversations with the professor, now took a hand in encouraging them. I sensed that a trap was being laid, but who was the predator and who the prey I couldn't decide.

One hot afternoon I was in the professor's study sorting through a stack of index cards. I became aware of soft footsteps in the hall, and I imagined that Frau Schissler had come back to the house for some forgotten parcel or soup bone. I was surprised, though, to hear the professor's bedroom door open and close; Frau Schissler knew it was his custom to sleep at that hour and wouldn't have thought of disturbing him. The clock downstairs in the parlor was just striking two.

I heard the professor cough, so I knew he'd lit a cigarette, but the other person—a woman, I was sure—seemed to be doing most of the talking. As the clock gonged the first quarter after the hour, the door opened again. A moment passed. Then, downstairs, the front door slammed with such force that it shook the house and everything in it. Dante Alighieri departed from his nail and crashed to the floor.

I rushed to the window and peered down at the front garden. There was Charlotte, dressed in leather trousers and an oatmeal-colored open weave shirt. An orange scarf covered her hair. What can she have been up to? I wondered and in the next instant understood perfectly well what she'd been up to. She mounted a bicycle—Gregorio's—and rode away, wobbling, as though long out of the habit of riding bicycles.

So this is what the terrible wild goose chase has driven Gregorio to, I thought. I wasn't sure whom I blamed more for the fiasco, him or Professor Zoppi.

I became aware of the professor's arthritic shuffle in the hall, and he appeared in the study doorway, wearing the ratty paisley dressing gown that looked prewar, pre any war you might care to mention. Calmly he surveyed the wreckage of broken glass and splintered frame. Dante scowled up from the floor, still disapproving. Too stunned to say anything, I remained by the window. "Alas," the professor said, "I am unable to help your friend." He shrugged, the matter closed as far as he was concerned. "Please don't invite him here again. As I explained, I have no influence."

Gregorio and I remained friends for a while, and I tried to forgive him for serving his wife up like a dozen oysters or a chestnut torte, but I couldn't pretend nothing had changed. By unspoken agreement we avoided discussing his poems and anything to do with Professor Zoppi, with the result that our conversations lagged. Meanwhile, I had made other friends in Bellinzona—Mick, an Australian slowly making his way around the world; Quentin and Suki, an expatriate couple from L.A.; a German botanist named Ilmar—and gradually I stopped dropping in at the bookstore. Once, sitting in a café with my friends near the Chiesa San Biagio, I glanced out the window and saw hurrying by on the sidewalk a pregnant woman who might have been Charlotte. Or not.

Soon afterward, on a day when November rain was turning the front garden into a slough, the professor completed his manuscript. I had anticipated a shout of triumph and the opening of a bottle of champagne when he reached the end, perhaps a toast to me as his invaluable assistant. None of that happened. When I'd typed the final page, he wrapped the manuscript in brown butcher's paper, tied the parcel with string, and addressed it to the university press in Michigan that had expressed a cautious interest in publishing it. Then he went to his room for his afternoon nap. Feeling vaguely deflated, I carried the bundle on the tram to the *ufficio postale centrale*. As I handed the manuscript over to the clerk, I sensed that I wouldn't be long in following it to the U.S. And indeed, within days, the professor began to hint that although he was happy to have me stay in Bellinzona, it might be time for me to proceed with my life.

The night before I took the train to Milan to begin my journey home, we sat at the kitchen table over one last *zuppa di fagioli*. It was now or never for an explanation, I figured. Emboldened by several glasses of the local Merlot, I asked why he had allowed Gregorio to continue on his lunatic course, tinkering with his poems until they no longer made a scrap of sense, to the writer or anyone else.

The professor pondered for a moment, wiping his mouth with the big striped napkin that he'd tied around his neck like a bib. Then he said, smiling wryly, "Oh . . . perhaps it was nothing more than an old man's mischief."

How very unkind, I thought. Even after Gregorio's willful self-humiliation, I felt resentment on his behalf. And wait just a minute here. Gregorio had expected to be transformed by Lazarro Zoppi—but so had I. He'd yearned for the professor's laurels to rub off on him. Me, too. Hadn't the old man misled us both? Research assistant, phooey. Menial gofer was all I'd been, about as much glory attached to the job as to my father's concrete-pouring, my mother's cafeteria meatloaf. I remembered all the pages typed, meals cooked, mislaid possessions located, with scarcely a word of thanks. He'd strung me along just as he had Gregorio.

I pushed aside my soup bowl and it thumped against the bread-board. "Gregorio wasn't only trying to curry favor," I said. "He truly wanted to learn from you."

"I tried to teach him."

"Really?" The professor pursed his lips, but let me go on. "Gregorio was so sure there was a trick to the writing, if only he could find it. *Il trucco,* was the word he used. If only you would help him."

But that, I thought bitterly, would be giving more of yourself than you were willing. Or knew how.

I wanted to leave the table and go upstairs to finish packing. However, something—perhaps the sober, almost sorrowful expression on the professor's face—kept me planted in my chair. For a long time the kitchen was silent. I could hear the dripping of the tap into the stone sink, the deliberate ticking of the clock in the parlor down the hall. Then the professor leaned across the table and laid his bony fingers on my arm.

"*Cara* Cecilia," he said gently. "In making poems, as in living, *non c'è trucco.* There is no trick, no secret, no shortcut. You must find your way yourself. That is what your friend had to learn, as we all must."

NERVE-WRACKIN' CHRISTMAS

Naomi watched her brother maneuvering Marilyn out of the display window, easing his skinny rear end past a jumble of mini-spotlights and a pyramid of TVs playing *Some Like It Hot.* Dixieland jazz rattled from every set. Suddenly Naomi realized that an extension cord threatened to tangle itself around Soren's leg. "Hold it," she said. She reached over to yank the cord out of its socket, and the cord snapped in her hand, stunning her with a bolt of electricity. Naomi staggered backward. Her ring glowed, on fire, and she flung it off onto the carpet.

Soren crouched in the window, Marilyn's torso in his arms, her plastic limbs splayed beneath a dusty cellophane gown. "Yikes," he said. "Look at your hand." It was scorched black. "Should I call 911?" he asked, clambering down from the window.

"I guess there isn't much point," Naomi replied, "since I seem to have survived." A blister had begun to rise on her finger where the ring had been. Warily, in case it might still harbor a charge, she picked the ring up from the floor.

"It's melted," Soren said in awe. In fact, the ring, a silver band engraved with ivy leaves that were supposed to represent eternal faithfulness, or something like that, looked as if it had been ground briefly in a garbage disposal—misshapen, chewed at the edges. "Didn't Gary give you that ring?"

"You know perfectly well Gary gave me that ring."

"It's a *sign,*" Soren pronounced. Her brother, who cultivated a cadaverous New York look and bristled with piercings here and there, was home in Annapolis between semesters at photography school, annoying their parents and Naomi's boyfriend and making a general pest of himself. To assuage his ennui he'd volunteered to create a new outfit for Marilyn, the signature centerpiece of the store's display window.

"You wish," Naomi replied. "Luckily, however, this isn't the Old Testament."

She went to the bathroom in back to scrub the scorch marks off, without a lot of success. The welt on her finger hurt more now. In a few minutes she heard Soren hauling Marilyn out the door, her limbs colliding with the jamb, the bell clanging feverishly. "Ciao," he yelled. When Naomi returned to the front a customer came in and began to peruse the film noir videos. She slipped the ring into a drawer behind the counter.

Gary took one look at the Classical section and groaned. Bach's *B Minor Mass* in the Beethoven category, Prokofiev mixed up with Puccini, the whole scene total chaos. He hated Christmas, which every year drove hordes of jerks to rifle through the CDs in a frenzy. Bad enough what they did to Country-Western, and to R&B and Soul, but Classical was always the worst. Those heads-in-the-clouds types couldn't even get it together enough to focus on the goddamn alphabet.

His feet were sore, his neck had a crick in it, the inane music blaring from the speakers was driving him nuts. While he straightened the racks Gary thought about how the landlord had just jacked up the rent on his condo, as good as wiping out the raise he'd received when promoted to assistant manager. Some promotion. All it meant was more problems dumped in your lap from both ends of the hierarchy.

Gary thought about the crumbling exhaust system on the Taurus—the car sounded like a Bradley Fighting Vehicle, only without the muscle. Somehow he was going to have to find the money to replace the exhaust. Face it, the whole damn car was falling apart chunk by chunk.

Moving Menotti's one-act operas out of the Mendelssohn slot, he thought about the phonecalls from his mom out in Waukesha. *Why can't you and Naomi come for Christmas? Surely you can take a few days off.*

Mom, listen to me. Tower Records never shuts down. It's like a hospital. Or the Army.

Gary did not have the guts to admit to his mother, who had trouble grasping the fine points of his relationship with Naomi, that his job wasn't the sole reason he couldn't go home for Christmas. "Waukesha?" Naomi had said, laughing, like he was proposing a jaunt down the Zambezi in a dugout. So he'd abandoned that idea. No way was he about to hand that brother of hers any more ammunition: *Nyah, nyah, mama's boy, pushing-thirty mama's boy.* Seemed like the kid was always underfoot, dropping by to sneer at Gary's collection of Dallas Cowboys souvenirs while deigning to drink Gary's beer, and Naomi did nothing to discourage the obnoxious brat.

Gary went to the back of the store, popped *Nerve-Wrackin' Christmas, Vol. 2* out of the CD player, and buried it in the trash barrel among a heap of Styrofoam peanuts.

On Sunday Naomi and her brother met for brunch at McGarvey's, down by the waterfront. Nearly drowned out by the clatter of talk and clanking of silverware, Bing Crosby was dreaming of a white Christmas. Fat chance. In this town a chilly drizzle was the best you could expect.

Investigating the construction of his tofu and artichoke lasagna, Soren asked, "So what did Gary say when you told him about the ring?" Soren was wearing a skimpy black suit jacket, a recent find at Junque Boutique, over a white T-shirt.

"I didn't."

"He didn't notice your hand?"

"He noticed, all right. He gave me a lecture about the perils of antiquated wiring and the folly of trusting predacious landlords." She cut a fried oyster in half.

"Neither of which has one iota to do with the extension cord."

"But it was sweet of him to be so concerned."

"Uh-huh."

Pensively Naomi chewed her oyster. "What kind of bugged me, though, was his assumption that the whole episode was somehow my fault."

His brows raised, Soren speared a mushroom. Just behind him, a waitress was shoving through the crowd at the bar, a tray of beer glasses balanced high above her head.

"My fault and yours, that is."

"Mine?" he croaked. "Precisely how did he arrive at that conclusion?"

"You were there, weren't you?"

"Geez, even my powers don't include zapping people with lightning bolts."

Naomi wasn't so sure about that, though Soren's methods of manipulation were usually more subtle.

"But *somebody* may be trying to tell you something," Soren went on. "Encouraging you to give this Gary thing a second thought."

This Gary thing. Naomi remembered last summer's trip to Quebec in the old Taurus, and their coming upon the ring in that charming shop in the Quartier Petit-Champlain, and Gary's endearingly hopeless attempts to speak French to the proprietor. What fun they'd had. They seemed so right for each other, both connected with the arts, sort of, both partial to Ben & Jerry's Aloha Macadamia ice cream. The trip was before she moved into Gary's condo, before she became aware of his odd little habits, like cutting cents-off coupons out of the Sunday paper before reading even the sports section, or asking guests to remove their shoes before approaching the wall-to-wall carpeting. Then there was all the time he spent on the phone with his bossy mother. "Give it a rest, Soren."

"You don't have to bite my head off."

"I happen to love Gary."

"Okay, okay. *A chacun son goût.*"

To accompany his lasagna Soren had ordered a champagne cocktail—a drink that seemed to be currently fashionable in his set, the result of spending too much time watching old Charles Boyer movies—which was no doubt, Naomi thought, going to wind up on her credit card.

"Anyhow, why didn't you tell him what happened to the ring?" he asked.

"I couldn't bring myself to do it. Even Gary would be upset at the symbolism, although there isn't any."

"Yeah, right."

"I told him I left the ring in the shop, on account of the blister on my finger."

"He bought that?"

"Temporarily. But sooner or later I'm going to have to explain why I'm not wearing it."

Soren grinned. "It could happen to fall down a grate. You could arrange for the store to be broken into and selected valuable items stolen. You could fly to Aruba on a package holiday and meet a guy who isn't a penny-pinching, judgmental, anal stick-in-the mud, like some we might mention."

"All those ideas are really cool, Soren. I'm so grateful for your advice."

Soren signaled the waitress to bring him another champagne cocktail.

In bed Gary held Naomi's hand, reassuring himself that the burn blister was pretty well healed, but aware of the absence of the silver ring. He decided he wasn't going to say a word about it, let her be the one to bring the subject up.

She snuffled in her sleep and turned over, her hand slipping from his. The bedroom was nearly dark, lit only by the glow of the streetlight seeping around the edges of the mini-blinds. He could just make out the mushroom shape of the Tiffany lamp on her dresser and the pile of her clothes tossed sloppily over a chair. The heap looked like a drunken body or a corpse. Naomi never hung up her clothes when she took them off and then wondered why she was always having to pay the cleaner outrageous prices to have them pressed, which wouldn't be so bad if her shop was actually making a profit. He hadn't lived with a girl before, not even a sister, so he had no one to compare her behavior to—except his mother, and Naomi wasn't a bit like his mother.

He loved Naomi, he was pretty sure he did, but he wished she'd be more responsible about things. Keep her wits about her, as his mom would say. Naomi's whole family was kind of dizzy when you came down to it. Her old man, a disheveled philosophy professor who tormented the cat and any visitors by playing Hindemith on a viola, would never have been able to support a family—let alone afford that house on Duke of Gloucester Street—if money hadn't been trickling down from some ancestral source that no one, including Naomi, ever mentioned. Not a lot of dough, just enough to insulate the family from harsh reality. Naomi's mother dabbled in useless things like origami and yoga and book discussion groups, and her brother . . . Gary wasn't even going to begin thinking about that little shithead or his adrenaline would start to flow, and he had to get some sleep. Tomorrow was going to be another harrowing day. Unlike Naomi, he didn't have the luxury of being able to show up for work an hour late and barely conscious—or not at all, as the spirit moved her.

But the more he lay there, worrying about how exhausted he was going to be in the morning, the more agitated and wakeful Gary became. All at once it occurred to him that maybe Naomi wasn't just being careless or forgetful, leaving the ring in her odds-and-ends drawer at the shop. What if her failure to put it on again was a big fat hint that up to now he had missed? Supposing she wasn't willing to settle for a modestly priced silver pre-engagement ring (bought with Canadian dollars) anymore? Supposing she expected the real thing, and not from Kwality Discount Jeweler's, either? He'd seen the hunk of ice her girlfriend Claire was sporting. How was he going to afford a ring like that, even on E-Z credit?

Gary got out of bed, made himself a peanut butter sandwich, and turned on the TV in the living room. He watched a black-and-white Jimmy Stewart movie, which was set in Budapest for some reason, until he fell asleep in his chair.

It might not be such a bad idea, Naomi thought, to have the ring mysteriously disappear, down a grate or wherever. A ring is only a material object, and whatever symbolic or sentimental meaning it carries can easily be reassigned, if necessary. Moreover, something about the damaged ring nagged at her. All week, every time Naomi opened the drawer to retrieve a pen or a Post-it, the sight of the ring gave her a queasy feeling deep in her gut, reminding her of the unpleasant surprise of the electric jolt, the reflexive way she'd flung the ring away from her, the lingering smell of scorched skin and metal. Not that she was superstitious, she told herself. Not that she believed for one second that what had happened was an omen, in spite of what Soren had said, in spite of Soren's uncanny way of being right about things like that.

Although the shop was busier than usual, customers picking up crime and action movies to see them through the Christmas festivities, she couldn't get the ring out of her mind. Her thumb kept feeling out the slightly sensitive place on her finger where it had been.

During a lull, shortly after two, Naomi put the ring into her coat pocket. She locked up, pointing the hands of the cardboard "I shall return" clock to 2:30. Past the display window with the newly gowned and coifed Marilyn she walked, past the antique shop that specialized in marine artifacts, and the Persian rug store, and the café that played Paul Winter in unending loops, around the corner to Prince George Street. At the end of the block she crossed College Avenue and entered the campus, empty at this time of year. Dead grass under her feet crunched with frost. Behind abandoned classroom buildings and dormitories the ground sloped down to soggy brown athletic fields and then to the river. Her boots were getting muddy, sinking into the turf.

At the river's edge, Naomi took the ring out of her pocket and, without pausing for even a moment's reflection, threw it high over the water. She waited for the *plink* but never heard it. Perhaps, she thought, the ring didn't fall at all, but instead was sailing toward the moon or a distant star—propelled by some force from inside herself, miraculously whole again, but no longer hers.

Naomi felt so happy, so downright ecstatic, that when Gary came around to the shop in the late afternoon bearing a small white velvet box, she just shook her head no. They went to McGarvey's to celebrate.

SINCE YOU'VE BEEN GONE

We had to wear white shoes with rubber soles, so I went downtown to Lawson's on Main Street and bought a pair on sale, but they didn't fit me right. They pinched my toes and chewed blisters into my heels and tormented my metatarsals. I hobbled around wincing until finally Ginny said, "Why you keep on wearing 'em? Those shoes killing your feet like that. You ain't so poor you can't afford another pair." For some reason, though, I never did get rid of those shoes.

During breaks between classes we sat together in the cafeteria, the four of us crowded around a table cluttered with med-surge textbooks and Styrofoam food containers, Aretha Franklin or The Temptations or Dionne Warwick on the jukebox. *I say a little prayer for you, I say a little prayer for you . . .*

We moaned over the math problems in pharmacology. If you didn't pass pharmacology you were out on your ear. We moaned even more about our supervisor, Miss Titley. Ginny claimed Miss Titley's heart was actually a plasma bag filled with sawdust. In Sondra's opinion our uniforms weren't designed for a human person, hers hung like a sack on her, and look how tight Ginny's was in the armpits. Mrs. McElroy said Sondra was absolutely right and we ought to get up a petition. Mrs. McElroy was always experimenting with her cap, taking it apart and trying to refold it into a more flattering shape, which never worked. Each attempt we hooted at, but she didn't give up.

One day Ginny told us that at home the night before she'd sat down to play the piano, whereupon a shotgun inside the piano bench went off and blew a hole in the wall.

"Jesus, Mary, and Joseph," Mrs. McElroy said.

Calmly Sondra scraped the chili off her chili dog.

"How'd the gun get in the piano bench?" I asked, fascinated and horrified at the kinds of things that could happen over in Parole, the colored section, where Ginny and her husband and various other relatives lived with Ginny's mother. Though I'd grown up in the town, I'd had no reason to venture very far out West Street, with its boarded-up storefronts and trash on the sidewalk. Parole was practically a foreign country, so far as I was concerned.

"Momma suspect Cousin Eldon." Ginny laughed her throaty laugh you could hear all over the cafeteria. "Cousin Eldon ain't talking."

Mrs. McElroy was forty-two years old and the mother of seven children, most of them still at home. She'd brag about being pure Irish on both sides back to Fin McCool. Sondra lived in Parole, like Ginny, but she had more white in her than negro. Her skin had a yellowish tinge and was dotted with freckles. Once when we were in the ladies' room and she was struggling to fix her hair, I asked her why she didn't just grow an Afro. In the mirror she smiled at me as if she'd never heard such a dumb question. Ginny was almost as black as the leather coat she wore, with a broad face and generous mouth. She'd gotten married in the summer, right before our course started at the community college, to a boy her same age, eighteen. His name was Fernald, and he had a job working for Baltimore Light and Electric.

From the beginning I felt drawn to Ginny's energy and good humor, but I couldn't help being aware of her strange smell, oily-sweet with a hint of something like parsnips, and the fact that her palms were so much lighter than the rest of her, except for the creases. The first time she touched me, laying her hand on my bare arm as she told a funny story, I felt a little odd about it. I hoped she didn't see that in my face.

We soon learned all kinds of things about each other. For instance, in October the McElroys couldn't scrape together the rent, and the kids had to pitch in their paper route money. Ginny seemed to have even more relatives than Mrs. McElroy, and they wandered in and out of her life in an amazingly random way. Ginny's cousin Eldon had arrived from Newark with a mouthful of teeth broken when the cops fire-hosed him during a "demonstration." "Riot, more like it," Ginny said. Her secret dream, she confided, was for her and Fernald to have a little place of their own, near Back Creek, so he could go crabbing whenever he wanted. She showed us her bankbook and the entries made every week when Fernald got his check from B.L.E. Sondra had a dream, too, to move to California after we graduated. No, her boyfriend would not be tagging along. He might be good-looking, Sondra said, but his lack of gumption doomed him to operate a Fry-O-Lator forever. The three of them knew about my crush on the guy who worked in Willetts Records, hopeless because he wore a wedding ring, and my painful menstrual periods, and my perpetual cold war with my mother.

Familiar though we were with intimate details of each other's lives, we never laid eyes on the insides of each other's houses. I could only imagine Ginny's momma's piano and the hole in the wall above the sofa where Cousin Eldon slept. On the days we trained in South Baltimore hospital I picked up Mrs. McElroy at her place, but I wasn't invited into her little cape, and I didn't even try to picture where she stowed all those kids. Tuesday and Thursday mornings. Ginny and Sondra would be waiting for us at a bus stop out on the highway, and the four of us would drive the thirty miles up to Baltimore in my '58 Chevy Bel Air that had its driver door held on with duct tape, the defroster blasting and Motown on the radio and the dawn bleaching out the sky. They chipped in for gas.

Mr. Lumb lay curled like a wrinkled black snail, urine the color of Murphy Oil Soap trickling into a plastic bag attached to the bed rail. He was a crabby old farmer from Prince Georges County who chewed tobacco, which was definitely a no-no on the floor, so he'd try to hide the plug from the nurses by stuffing it under his pillow. Mr. Lumb had a million things wrong with him: diabetes, ileitis, prostatitis, and congestive heart failure, for starters. By rights he should have been dead long ago, but Ginny figured God didn't need Mr. Lumb up there complaining about the racket from the harps and lyres and the glare off the pearly gates. God could manage without Mr. Lumb for a while, she said, and in the meantime, I'd got him. He didn't have a tooth in his head. Plus, all the meds he was on made him foggy in the brain. Mean foggy. Plus, that Prince Georges dialect might as well have been Mongolian, for all I could decipher it. When Mr. Lumb punched the call bell to order me to do something, which he did about twenty times per shift, my confusion didn't make his disposition any sweeter.

That day we were short-handed, since the one orderly assigned to the floor was out sick and there were four or five new admissions and a cardiac patient arrested in room 411. When there's a Code Blue most of the nurses on the floor have to respond—the real nurses, that is. Now that I'd given Mr. Lumb his sponge bath, I would have to change his linen by myself. Mr. Lumb was surprisingly heavy considering he had hardly any flesh on his old bones: a dead weight because he refused to cooperate. A long plastic tube entered his body and another one exited it, and I hadn't yet fully got the hang of maneuvering those appendages when moving a patient in the bed.

I half-lifted, half-dragged Mr. Lumb to the far side of the bed so I could slip the soiled sheet from beneath him. Just as I began to ease the fresh one under him, his IV needle yanked out of his skinny old arm. Mr. Lumb's eyes glittered with rage and he started to mutter something, probably conjuring a curse on me and my entire family. Earlier that morning the resident, Dr. Sharkey, had spent half an hour puncturing Mr. Lumb in one spot or another until he found a vein that wouldn't collapse. Now the hunt would have to begin all over again.

On Tuesday the Shark had bitten my head off for almost contaminating his sterile field during a procedure, although I hadn't come anywhere near it. Picturing what was in store for me when the Shark found out about the IV, I began to cry, and that's when Ginny poked her head in the door.

"You need a hand? I'm done with my lady in 403." She came in and shut the door behind her. "Hey, girl, what you blubbering for?"

"I pulled out Mr. Lumb's IV by mistake."

"Uh-uh-uh," Ginny said sympathetically.

"The Shark's going to report me to Miss Titley."

"Before he kills you or after?"

"Oh, Ginny," I wailed.

"The Shark ain't gonna do neither one, 'cause I'm gonna tell him the mean ole bastard did it hisself, just to get us in trouble."

"You can't lie for me, Ginny."

"Wait and see if I can't."

I wondered if I'd have the courage to do the same for her, and that made me feel bad. I looked down at Mr. Lumb. Part of him lay on a dirty sheet and part on a clean one, all of him mad as a hornet. "What if he tells?"

They could probably hear her laugh all the way down at the nurses' station. "Nobody around here understand a word that ole man say, 'cept me. Fernald's momma born and raised in Prince Georges County."

We four were the class oddballs, and I suppose that's what brought us together in the first place. Mrs. McElroy, used to bossing seven kids around, wasn't about to bow and scrape to Miss Titley. Nobody else in our class had kids at all, except for a guy who'd been a medic in Vietnam. Ginny was a vegetarian and could play Chopin as well as a spectacular game of Ping-Pong. She made fun of the other black girls, with their polished shoes and pressed uniforms and starched caps pinned grimly to straightened hair. "Nigger Florence Nightingales" she called them once, shocking me. Sondra didn't fit in with those girls, either. "Uppity high yeller," I overheard one of them say about her. As for me, I wasn't at all sure I wanted to be a nurse to begin with. The whole thing had been my mother's idea. "You'll always have a way to earn your living," she said, as if she had her doubts that any man was going to volunteer to earn it for me. "Pain and suffering will never go out of style." But I was clumsy. Mrs. McElroy and Ginny and Sondra were turning hospital corners with the speed and finesse of croupiers in a casino when I still had trouble getting the sheet even on the mattress.

So they helped me out with the practical stuff, and I drummed enough math into their heads to get them through pharmacology. We felt like it was us against Miss Titley and the Shark and the whole rest of the world.

In December, right after exams, an ice storm created a lot of havoc in town, including freezing the Chevy's tires onto the street outside my house as if they'd been welded to the pavement. The storm also uprooted an oak tree that had stood in front of the Governor's Mansion for at least two hundred years. First thing the next morning Baltimore Light and Electric dispatched a crew to saw the tree's limbs off, and one of the members of the crew was Ginny's husband, Fernald. According to the item that appeared two days later in the back of the paper, the branch Fernald was working on must have got snagged on the line. He reached too far out of the bucket trying to jiggle it loose, and a guide rope tangled around his neck as he fell. There he was, dangling from a rope fifteen feet above the sidewalk, and none of the other guys on the crew, or the governor's staff, or the governor's wife, or Spiro himself, noticed what was happening. Finally a man out walking his dog spotted him and raised the alarm.

The paper also carried Fernald's funeral announcement, but I didn't know if I should go. Ginny and I were friends. We'd practiced taking blood pressures on each other until our arms were numb. In micro lab we'd pricked each other's fingers and squeezed out drops of blood to type, both of us O positive. We'd observed our first surgery together, a cholecystectomy, and though she appeared soberly attentive behind her mask, and I'm certain she was, I could also hear her saying, *Whooee, that one mess o' guts in there, look like a dog's breakfast,* and I forgot my fear of fainting across the incision.

Still, I couldn't decide if the experiences we'd shared made me the kind of friend that attends a person's husband's funeral. I called Mrs. McElroy to ask if she was going and she said she'd like to—what a tragedy, what a waste of a young life—but she had so much to do she could hardly see straight, Christmas right around the corner and all. At Sondra's nobody answered the phone.

The morning of the service, a Saturday, I felt a cold coming on.

Outside, a chill drizzle was making the ice and snow pucky. My mother kept nagging me to go to the laundromat and the grocery store. I couldn't get myself together enough even to feed my goldfish. The last thing I wanted was to go to that funeral, but I did.

The Dudley Street A.M.E. Church reeked of sweat and wet wool and the sickening perfume of more than a dozen gigantic bouquets on the altar. They must have had the furnace churning away full-blast. I looked around for Sondra among the hundreds of mourners that packed the place, but couldn't find her. Finally I sat in a pew next to a large elderly lady in a felt hat, and right away another large old lady, this one wearing a brown coat, shoved in beside me. Up front, in the middle of all those bouquets, was a bronze casket that looked like it had cost a fortune, and I thought of Ginny's bankbook with the money saved for their little house. After some singing and prayers, a man with a long gloomy face and round eyeglasses that reflected the ceiling light came to the pulpit. At first, suffocating between the two old ladies and dazed with virus, I didn't pay much attention to what the preacher was saying. After a while, though, his voice began to rise to a higher pitch. "Now the Lord come out of the *whirlwind!*" he suddenly shouted. I jolted awake. "And the Lord say to Job, 'Gird up your loins! You is a *man!*'"

"Amen!" cried the old lady in the brown coat.

"'Get out your glad rags and put 'em on!' He say. 'Put on your dancin' shoes!'"

The old lady pulled herself to her feet. "Praise the Lord!"

"'Let fly your anger! They who is puffed up with pride, *squash* 'em!'"

More people were on their feet now.

"'The wicked'—for a moment the preacher's eyes seemed to fix on me, light glinting off his spectacles—'the *wicked,* stomp on 'em right where they is at.'"

In his black gown the preacher glided down from the pulpit and approached the coffin. "Brother Fernald, just like the Lord made you, He made the Great Beast. The bones of the Beast be strong as brass, tough as bars of iron. His heart be hard like a millstone." The preacher laid both hands on the coffin. "Out of his mouth go burning lamps and sparks of *fire,*" he exclaimed, and I almost expected the coffin lid to spring open and the Great Beast to burst out like a jack-in-the-box, smoke seething from his nostrils. But then the preacher's voice dropped to a whisper and he shut his eyes. "Lord, You made the Great Beast and You made Brother Fernald. We know You can do all things. Now we see You face to face. We accept Your will."

"Amen," moaned the old lady in the felt hat.

The preacher returned to the pulpit and we bowed our heads to pray. *For all our days pass away under thy wrath, our years come to an end like a sigh.* The lady at the organ played music I vaguely recognized but couldn't have named, and the pallbearers hefted the coffin. They lurched toward the side door, followed by Ginny and her relatives, including a scrawny young man with a mustache who might have been Cousin Eldon. Then a bunch of girls—Ginny's cousins and friends, I guessed—crowded to the front of the church and picked up the wreaths and baskets of flowers. The old lady in the brown coat pushed me forward and before I knew what was happening thrust one of the baskets into my arms.

Those of us carrying the flowers traipsed behind Ginny down a flight of wooden steps and across the churchyard to the road. Her flower girls, I thought ridiculously, humiliated because I hadn't sent any myself, the idea had never occurred to me, and whoever had paid for these would think I was pretending to be the sort of friend I wasn't and couldn't be. We stumbled along the edge of the road, dead grass and litter under our feet, rain soaking our coats, traffic splashing by, all the way to the cemetery. The rest of the mourners came raggedly along behind us.

Then, with the other girls, I found myself putting down my basket next to a deep hole in the ground. Ginny had her face turned upward, into the cold rain. I knew she was seeing her young husband swinging by the neck.

When school started up again in January, our class was split apart into groups. Like before, classes met three days a week out at the community college, but on Tuesdays and Thursdays we drifted around the county learning about different aspects of public medicine. I drove over to Crownsville, the State Mental Hospital, to work with the nut cases. Sondra played blocks with autistic and Down syndrome kids in a facility connected somehow to the Maryland school system. Ginny and Mrs. McElroy were assigned to a clinic on Franklin Street. I heard from Mrs. McElroy that the black girls who went to the clinic for pre-natals, most of them unmarried, thought orange pop was a good source of vitamin C. She also told me that Ginny thought she was pregnant, or hoped she was, carrying her poor dead husband's child. But a week later it turned out Ginny wasn't pregnant, after all.

In class, Ginny sat in the back of the lecture hall with some other black nursing students. During breaks she hung out with those girls instead of joining Mrs. McElroy and Sondra and me at our table in the cafeteria. The jukebox played "I'm Wondering," "I Wish it Would Rain," "Sweet Sweet Baby Since You've Been Gone," "There Was a Time." Ginny's quarters, I figured. "Why that girl shunning us?" Sondra said, and Mrs. McElroy answered, "She needs to be sad. Leave her be." But I feared that Ginny scorned me for butting in on her husband's funeral and carrying one of her flower baskets when I had no right to, and that's why she avoided us. Maybe I was one of the people puffed up with pride that God told Job to squash. I thought of explaining to Ginny that it was the busybody old lady's fault for forc-ing me into it, but supposing Ginny hadn't even seen me? I'd feel like a fool apologizing for something she didn't know I'd done and wouldn't have cared two hoots about if she did. Better just keep quiet.

I hated Crownsville, and I missed Ginny, who would have found entertaining things to say about it, easing the misery of filthy green walls and stink and shrieking inmates. She'd have made Crownsville bearable, which I couldn't do on my own. February and March were cold and wet. I went on wearing those wretched shoes, which were probably doing permanent damage to my feet.

Nobody put any coins in the jukebox. One of our black classmates, the guy who'd been a medic in Vietnam, got up from his table and hurled the metal trash can lid to the linoleum and shoved the remains of his meal into the can and stomped out. Ginny came over and sat with us, because Sondra had her little transistor radio on. We listened to the announcer talking about fires in the ghettos of Chicago, Detroit, Newark, Boston, Baltimore. Federal troops ordered into D.C. Looting, brick-throwing, people shot dead. A few white shop-keepers. Mostly, black people shot dead. It didn't make sense to me. "Uh-uh-uh," Ginny said.

In those days I didn't read newspapers, except for the local paper. We never talked about politics at school. When, the night before, I heard on the TV news that Martin Luther King had been killed out-side his motel room in Memphis, it didn't mean much to me one way or the other.

"They fixin' to burn the whole country down," Ginny said. I couldn't tell if she was happy about that or not.

The four of us gathered our books and went out into April sun-shine. Walking across the parking lot, I thought I smelled smoke, but decided I was imagining it. A horde of students were waiting for the shuttle-bus—something must have happened to the bus or its sched-ule—so, for the first time in months, Sondra and Ginny climbed into the back of the Chevy. I crawled across the front seat, and Mrs. Mc-Elroy got in and shut the door. None of us said anything. I didn't turn on the radio.

As we drove south on Ritchie Highway we saw a dusky gray haze over the city, though it was way too early for dusk. The trees by the side of the road were a delicate feathery olive shade, and grass was greening up in open fields.

By the time we got to the bridge, no doubt about it, something big was on fire beyond us to our right, in the west side of the city. Clouds of smoke roiled into the sky. Even with the windows rolled up we could smell it, like burning tires. We heard a distant sound of sirens. "Holy mother of God," Mrs. McElroy said. She found a string of rosary beads in her purse. In the back seat, Ginny and Sondra were murmuring to each other in a private lingo even harder to understand than Mr. Lumb's. A crowd of people, mostly black, milled around the bus stop where I used to drop off Ginny and Sondra. I sailed right on by. "Hey," Ginny said. "Where you going?"

"I'm taking you home."

"You ain't gonna do no such of a thing," Ginny said. She grabbed my shoulder and gave it a shake.

"We'll let off Mrs. McElroy," I said, "and then we'll talk about it." She retreated, thumping her body against the rear seat back. I turned into the neighborhood of shabby one- and two-family houses where the McElroys lived, took a right and a left and a right, cutting corners, going well above the speed limit. The sky was gray, and flakes of ash drifted down onto the windshield like snow. I pulled up in front of the little cape that housed so many kids. Bikes and other toys littered the scrabbly lawn.

Before getting out of the car, Mrs. McElroy said to me under her breath, "Take them back to the bus stop. They'll be fine."

"She right about that," Ginny said.

"This is my car," I said, and I executed a fast U-turn that took us up the curb and a few feet over the McElroy lawn, narrowly missing a plastic kiddie vehicle and some kind of bush. "I'll make the decisions here."

"You think you so great 'cause you got a car?" Ginny said. The tires bumped back onto the pavement. "This sorry-ass car?" If the Chevy had come equipped with four doors, she'd have opened hers and leapt out, dragging Sondra with her. Unfortunately for her, she was stuck.

"You've been glad enough to ride in it," I said.

Ginny started in on a comeback but, displaying the first sign of anger I'd ever seen in her, Sondra told her to shush, and for the moment Ginny did. Back on Taylor I picked up speed and roared past the stadium. At the cemetery I made a right onto West Street, and now the billows of smoke were dead ahead of us, maybe a mile away. Sondra began to cough.

"Stop the car," Ginny said. "Now." There was a hardness in her voice I had never heard before. I pulled crookedly into a No Parking spot and switched off the ignition. The sirens were louder now. Somewhere vehicle horns were blaring.

"Listen up," Ginny said, right in my ear. "In case you too stupid to notice, you white." I wrenched my head around and we stared into each other's faces. I saw her broad African nose and the dark, nearly purple skin that up that close showed raised blemishes like tiny scars. "You white, and this ain't no fun and games."

"I'll keep the door locked."

"Huh," Ginny said. As if this tin can was going to save me from a mob of armed black men. I thought of Cousin Eldon and his shotgun.

"Let's go," Sondra said, leaning forward over the seat to open the passenger door.

"I'm afraid for you."

Ginny snorted. "We be fine, just like Mrs. McElroy say." She and Sondra climbed out of the Chevy and banged the door shut. Lugging their books in carry-bags, they set off on foot toward Parole, Ginny in her shiny black leather coat, Sondra with her thin hair limp on her neck.

I imagined Ginny suddenly turning around. I imagined her sprinting back to the car and rapping her knuckles on my side window. "Thanks for coming to the funeral," she'd shout through the glass. "It meant a lot to me."

But that didn't happen. They kept walking along the sidewalk, away from me, until I couldn't see them anymore.

Text design by Mary Sexton
Typesetting by Delmastype, Ann Arbor, Michigan
Font: Adobe Garamond

Claude Garamond's sixteenth-century types were modeled on
those of Venetian printers from the end of the previous century.
Adobe designer Robert Slimbach based his Adobe Garamond
roman typefaces on the original Garamond types, and based
his italics on types by Robert Granjon, a contemporary of
Garamond's. Slimbach's Adobe Garamond was released in 1989.

—courtesy www.adobe.com